To Lea

All our love
on your 21st

Mum, Dad & Sally xx
3.4.98.

A LITTLE SHAME

Patricia Lacy

MINERVA PRESS

LONDON

MONTREUX   LOS ANGELES   SYDNEY

ISBN 1 86106 829 8

First Published 1997 by
MINERVA PRESS
195 Knightsbridge
London SW7 1RE

Printed in Great Britain for Minerva Press

A LITTLE SHAME

Un paou de bergougno es leou passada.
(A little shame is soon over.)

Occitan proverb

Chapter One

Memory is a strange beast. You can train it not to follow you; you can ignore its whimperings until you are free of the knowledge of its existence. But when you return to the place where you left it, you will find it still there, waiting, relaxed, as if it had always known you would one day return. And the dormant beast rouses and shakes itself, facing you defiantly. You meet its accusing gaze and your whole being is reflected in its eyes. Then it attacks in all its fury.

It was Paul, my godson, now middle-aged, who had suggested I accompany him on a business trip to the southern states of Europe. It would be a leisurely, comfortable car-ride for an elderly lady who had once loved to travel, and it would make more of a break for him too. We had always been close, so I agreed to his invitation with eagerness, took delight in packing and set off on the first part of the journey through the Eurotunnel completed four decades before. It was January; there was little traffic and we made good time to Milan, Marseilles and Barcelona. Oh, the joys of waiting in city cafés for Paul and watching the world go by the windows. I had always taken pleasure in being the observer. The spectator sees most of the game, so they say.

The business deals completed, Paul was in jovial mood as we travelled back through France and in order to prolong the trip by a few hours turned the car off the motorway, heading into the Central Massif. It was then that I began to recognise place names, and after a while the very landscape became strangely familiar. An emotion stirred deep within me like a hunger needing to be satisfied, an anxiety needing to be calmed.

"I would like to go," I said, "to Saint-André-sur-Audan."

*

6

She had travelled by ferry and rail, the young woman with her suitcases, catching the night-train from Paris. She had reserved a top bunk in a compartment for six so that she could sit upright to read, and had room to put her luggage in the space over the door. The train had sped through the darkness, slowing and coming to a halt in the light of unknown stations where its imminent departure had been announced over loud-speakers to deserted platforms. A slight pull at her body had indicated that the train was moving off, sliding smoothly out of the station; the lights had reflected on the ceiling, crossing ever faster until darkness and speed had lulled her again into sleep. Earlier, she had asked the *contrôleur* to wake her at the stop before Pradoux where she was to alight shortly after seven, but having noticed the change of sound as the train passed over the long viaduct to get there she was already climbing down from her bunk when her call came. The next station would be hers. She had stood in the lighted corridor, looking out and seeing only the snow along the side of the track. When the train had eased to a halt, she had stepped down, dragging her suitcases out one by one on to the snow, and had slammed the door shut. The train had given a lurch and had slipped past, taking its familiar sounds into the darkness until she was aware of the silence.

She picked up her cases and made for the light. It came from a small building dividing the platform from the car-park outside. Under the lamp was "Pradoux", painted in white. She knocked the snow off her shoes on the wooden floor of the building, the noise taking on importance in the stillness.

No vehicle stood on the car-park. No lights were seen approaching. What if he did not come?

She remained standing by the door, the cold gradually penetrating the warmth she had borne with her from the train. As the black sky became lighter she distinguished a road going by the end of the car-park. She fixed her eyes on that point until she was rewarded at last by the sight of headlights, and the car itself, turning towards her. She moved forward as the car drew up.

The driver got out, unsmiling, and they shook hands. He had dark hair swept back, and a heavy moustache.

"Monsieur Rodez?"

"Albert."

"Helen Camberley."

Albert Rodez was the mayor. She knew that from Chantal's letter: "Albert Rodez will meet you at the station. He is the mayor of the village and has the Hotel de l'Audan. I hope that you will be happy to take my classes for two months. I am pleased to go to England. It is my ambition for a long time to teach in an English school." Chantal was already in Britain, spending the New Year with friends in Carlisle.

"The road was icy," said the man in French, by way of an explanation for his lateness, as they drove away from the station.

"Thank you for coming to fetch me."

"Did you have a good journey?"

"Yes, thank you, though I am tired after travelling all night."

"You can sleep after breakfast." He turned briefly and smiled, showing sudden charm.

They drove on in silence, up over the hills where the pale morning light now shone eerily on the expanses of snow. Without warning, the car swung to the side of the road and stopped. The young woman gave a cry. To the right, the ground fell away to a deep ravine where way, way below one could see wisps of cloud and a solitary bird with huge wings circling an outcrop of rocks; and below that, far below, was a river.

"That's the Audan," said the man, clearly satisfied by her reaction.

How different, how very different it all was from home. Here she was, amid the grandeur of a desolate landscape, and moreover with a man she did not know. It was all unreal, her journey through the night, her wait in the cold, the deep gorge. And now began the descent into the valley. They left the bleakness of the snow, winding down through the pine-forests until they came upon a village clinging to the rock-face and surrounded by its medieval walls.

"There you see Saint-André-sur-Audan," said the man. "You have arrived."

*

"I am writing to you because there are things you ought to know," he was to write some years later. "Things are no longer what they were." Were they ever what they were or only what they seemed to be? I stood with Paul at the spot where she had once cried out and I looked down at the ravine of time into what was, or what appeared to be.

*

She arrived new to the village, fresh, eager, without prejudice, to teach, to learn, to experience. Her life was neatly organised into a school timetable, a small flat at the College and people on hand to help her. The boundaries of her experience were to be as closely defined as the gorge which enclosed Saint-André-sur-Audan. She was secure, being driven into the village by the mayor himself, to be given breakfast, to sleep. She had indeed arrived.

A boy of about thirteen was sitting on the wall by the bridge with a stick in his hand. He waved it as the car approached and leaping down ran alongside, brandishing it and shouting in obvious delight, "Hello, hello." The woman smiled back and turned questioningly to the man.

"That's André."

"André?"

"My nephew." He spoke as if he expected her to know.

"Is he one of my pupils?"

"Of course."

The car pulled into the yard of the Hotel de l'Audan. They got out and already the boy was there, happy and awkward, to shake hands with this new teacher from England, to make her welcome. In practised English he asked her if she had had a good journey, if she had slept well on the train and if she would like breakfast. He amused and impressed her.

"You are called André?"

"Yes, miss."

"André of Saint-André-sur-Audan," she quipped.

"Of Mas Saint-André," the boy corrected her. "I'm from up there, on the Causse." He pointed up to land beyond the top of the ravine.

The luggage was taken inside. Three little girls in pyjamas ran up and kissed their father before shyly coming and kissing the stranger whom papa had met at the station. Madame Rodez, in her green dressing-gown, greeted her with a smile and a warm hand-shake. She was a thickset woman with straight hair and a pleasant face. After leaving instructions to André to serve breakfast to their guest, she hustled the three children out of the room and they could be heard scampering upstairs.

The boy proudly set before her a long loaf of fresh bread, some butter and a pot of runny strawberry jam. Then he carried a bowl of white coffee to the table, carefully, so as not to spill any. She took it, cupping her hands around it and drawing comfort from its warmth before she ever lifted it to drink. The boy watched her, smiling encouragement, asked if it was good and offered more.

Fatigue, combined with a sense of well-being, overcame her. She was led upstairs to be shown a bathroom and a room with a large bed and with shutters pulled to. The door was closed upon her and she slept.

It was past midday when she awoke. She padded across the polished wooden floor to open the shutters on to the view. Her window overlooked the Audan swirling green and clear as it rounded the steep mass of rock opposite. To the left she could see upstream where the Audan had cut deep into the narrow gorge. To the right, just down from the hotel, she could see the bridge arching elegantly over the river, seemingly fragile yet strong enough to withstand the massive flash-floods which had twice that century engulfed it. She was never to tire of that view during her two months' stay.

"The heating is good at the College during the week because of the boarders," explained Madame Rodez, over a lunch of pâté, salad and onion tart. "But on Friday they go home until Monday morning and the College is empty. Chantal Boileau always returns to her parents' house in Pradoux for the weekend. You can come here, as our guest."

"You are very kind."

"No, no. It is a pleasure for us. We are not busy now because the hotel is closed. During the winter we clean, we decorate, we prepare for the summer." She shrugged. "We can't offer you a lot but... would you like that?"

"Very much, thank you." The young woman smiled round the table. The little girls smiled back and even Albert Rodez acknowledged her appreciation. "Please call me Helen, won't you?"

"And I am Monique, my husband is Albert, as you know, and these are Anne Sophie, who's six, Laurence, four, and Nathalie, two."

There were more smiles.

"Has André left?"

She would have liked to have seen again the boy who had served her coffee, but he had returned home to Mas Saint-André on the Causse. His mother had come shopping to the village and had collected him.

"He likes being here," said Monique. "Last summer holidays he helped in the hotel, or played with his cousins. He stayed last night because he wanted to be the first pupil to see you."

"His English is very good."

She saw a look pass between husband and wife.

"That may be so," said Albert, closing the subject.

In the afternoon the principal of the College, M. Noiret, called in to welcome her and take her on a tour of the establishment. He was a stocky man of about fifty, with greying hair cut short, and merry eyes behind round spectacles.

The College dominated the village, being incorporated in the surrounding wall at the highest point up a steep slope. They got there by car, skirting the ramparts and approaching from above, through an archway. M. Noiret showed her first the flat which was to be hers. It was reached by a flight of stone steps near the arch and inside she found a bedroom overlooking it, a small shower-room and a living-room fitted as a kitchen at one end. The window there overlooked the upper part of the valley and on closer inspection she found it was built into the medieval walls which rose high above the narrow road they had just travelled up.

"I hope you like the flat," said M. Noiret.

"It's perfect."

"You'll stay at the hotel at weekends, did you know?"

"Yes, yes, that suits me very well. You are all very kind."

They went down the steps and M. Noiret handed her the key to the flat before unlocking the main building.

"I suppose Mademoiselle Boileau – Chantal – has told you about the College?"

"Yes. She said this was one of the smallest schools in France."

"And the best."

"Of course."

They walked the cold stone corridors and peered into empty classrooms with shuttered windows. The school without pupils was lifeless, meaningless. Her own classroom had posters of Britain around the walls, incongruous in their setting and decidedly foreign. A quick count showed eighteen chairs and tables for her largest class, there being only fifty-one pupils shared between the four year groups. Where did André sit?

She found out two days later when the Spring term started. For each lesson she was faced with a group of bright-eyed, eager children all wanting to communicate with their new teacher and to please her.

Of all her pupils André was the most sensitive, showing his approval, giving her confidence and finding pretexts to speak to her afterwards. He was a handsome child, with black, wavy hair swept back in a style not unlike his uncle's, black eyebrows and lashes but with intense blue eyes.

When she had no lessons she was free to do as she pleased. Her timetable was such that she invariably had some free time in the mornings and a good deal of free time in the afternoons. She always had lunch at the College, enjoying the meals prepared by the chef whose Paris diplomas were a matter of pride not just for him but for the College in general. Besides, it was the only time she could meet other members of staff.

Sometimes she spent her time in her own classroom, preparing or marking work. At other times she went back to her flat to read the mail from home, or she wandered down to the shops. Apart from the little post office, there were four shops: the bureau de tabac which was open all hours; the bakers, which opened most mornings; the mini-supermarket which opened as and when the owner felt like it; and the butchers which was open at any time because the owners liked people to drop in for a chat. All the other shops were boarded up for the winter and the riverside cafés and restaurants were stacked high with tables and chairs within their glass façades.

The visits to the shops took time as she was supposed to make both purchases and conversation and the young woman delighted in this, knowing she was different, special, for it was not the tourist season, but also believing she was accepted, as one of the village, sharing their winter. Everyone knew who she was, where she came from, where she was living. As she explored the old village, with its maze of narrow, cobbled alleys and tunnels and flights of steps, she was greeted by anyone she chanced to meet, though seeing, even hearing anyone, was rare.

"You are not too bored?" the old priest used to ask whenever their paths crossed. Oh, no, she was never bored. There was so much still to discover.

Chapter Two

One evening Albert drove her up to Mas Saint-André for apéritifs with André's parents, Philippe and Sylvie Massaud, while the children stayed with Monique. The latter was, she discovered, Sylvie's younger sister. In her mind she had related Albert and André's mother. Mas Saint-André consisted of a cluster of stone houses on the bleak plateau with the Massaud home, an old farmhouse, set apart. As the car pulled up outside, the family stood by the door to greet them.

Sylvie was beautiful, finely featured and with long, dark, curly hair clasped loosely back, allowing strands to escape and frame her face. She stood with her hand on André's shoulder. Philippe was also dark, with those same blue eyes as André, and a beard making his thin face appear even longer.

They welcomed her civilly, invited her to take a seat by the log fire burning in the stone fireplace and offered drinks and salt biscuits. The conversation took a conventional pattern with which she had grown familiar: did she like the area, the village, the College? Her responses, though positive, brought cross-glances between the other three.

"Do you think, mademoiselle, that English is a relevant subject at the College?" asked Philippe.

"Don't start, darling," put in Sylvie sharply. "Not now."

"Of course. The pupils are happy to learn," said the young woman, "and English is used widely in the world."

"That is not what I meant, but no matter."

"André, you enjoy English, don't you?" She turned to the boy for support.

He hesitated, however, as if considering the enormity of the question, and she was mortified.

"My son enjoys all his lessons, don't you, my darling?"

"Yes, Mother."

There was a silence in which the woman felt ill at ease and, for the first time since her arrival in France, an outsider.

"It is interesting to visit a farm," she said to open up a new subject.

"One can hardly call it a farm any more," said Sylvie.

"We have the sheep," Philippe remarked. "Not to mention a pig."

"A few sheep and a pig no longer make a farm. My husband does other work. He helps the builder and mends roofs. I would like to open a little restaurant here in summer, but my husband..." She tailed off.

Philippe turned and said as if apologetically, "I don't like tourists. They destroy what they come to find." He directed a dark look at Albert.

"Let's not get into local politics," said Albert quietly. "Now, Helen, tell us about your life back home."

She was grateful to be offered a safe subject and chatted happily for a few minutes.

The log on the fire shifted. Sylvie reached forward with a poker and prodded it, sending a rush of sparks up the chimney.

"We need more logs," said Sylvie to Philippe.

"I'll go presently."

Sylvie suddenly stood up and walked over to the door. "Come and help me, Albert."

"I said I'd go." Philippe did not disguise his annoyance.

"Yes, presently, you said. It's always presently and never now. We need more logs now. Come on, Albert."

"It's okay, Philippe, I don't mind going."

Albert followed Sylvie and the door shut behind them. She was left with the boy and Philippe who were both staring into the glow of the fire. An old wall-clock ticked away the seconds.

A tabby cat had entered the room as the others left and it came and leaped straight on to the young woman's lap, settling down with its head towards the fire. She took comfort from stroking it, fondling its unusually long ears and gently rubbing its cheeks. It stretched out a paw contentedly.

"What's its name?" she asked André.

"We just call it Minet."

There was silence again and the clock ticked on.

"Another drink, mademoiselle?" asked Philippe at last, turning his blue eyes on her.

"No, thank you. It's very nice but I'd better not. I'm not really used to it."

"Ah, the English. You would perhaps prefer a cup of tea?" He grinned, almost as boyishly as his son.

"No, no thanks. Really." She smiled back.

"I apologise if my question about English as a subject made you uncomfortable. It was impolite of me."

"Not at all."

"Oh yes, I was implying that English shouldn't be taught, wasn't I?"

"Maybe. Yet the fact is that it is."

Philippe sighed. "We must talk about this sometime. Not now, but sometime. Would you mind?"

"No, of course not. It interests me."

"But not now." Philippe nodded towards his son.

She understood and went on, "Have you always lived in Mas Saint-André?"

"Me, my parents and my grandparents before me."

"And your great-grandparents and your great-great-grandparents," chanted André, joining in.

"Not my wife. Her family comes from Pradoux. As for my son," He reached over and patted André's shoulder, "as for him..." he turned back and gazed into the fire, "... we'll see."

Another subject of conversation had led to an impasse. She searched for something to say and stopped herself just in time from the indiscretion of making an appreciative comment about the comfort of an open fire. She turned her attention back to the cat for a while, then looked across at André. Was this really the same boy who had run alongside the car to welcome her? Was it really he who had served the coffee so carefully or who had been so smilingly attentive in class?

The boy sensed her gaze and returned it, lingering a few moments, as if understanding, to reassure her. She relaxed. All was well.

Sylvie and Albert returned with the logs, cutting through the ambience the others had shared. Sylvie stacked the logs by the hearth and dropped one on to the fire. Flames crept up from the embers, fingering the wood playfully at first, but afterwards clutching at it possessively. The wood spat and crackled, then settled back and blazed, giving off such heat that Philippe had to push his chair back.

Albert helped himself to another drink and refilled Sylvie's glass. Before she accepted it she spotted the cat asleep on the young woman's lap.

"Ah, my cat, my Minet. He is disturbing you."

The young woman protested in vain; the cat was scooped up into Sylvie's arms and placed firmly on her own lap. The cat, restive, was stroked heavily until it stayed of its own accord. Only then did Sylvie accept her glass from Albert.

"So," said Albert to Philippe, "it's time to kill the pig again."

"It's on the cards for next week. Will you come?"

"Of course, to help on the day and to Sunday lunch as usual, if that still suits you."

Philippe turned to the woman. "We would like you to come too, mademoiselle."

"Not to help with the killing, I hope," she replied, in fun. She had heard the squeals of a pig from her flat one day and later on wandering out through the archway of the College had come across a neighbour cutting up his pig just beyond the village walls. Entrails hung from the lower branches of a nearby plane tree.

"Good gracious, no," cried Sylvie, shocked, not seeing the woman was joking. "But if you come a week on Sunday with my sister and my brother-in-law – and the children, naturally – you will eat some fine pork."

"And black pudding," added André, his face bright in anticipation of the feast.

Arrangements were made amicably between Albert and Philippe, goodbyes were said and the family stood at the door, Sylvie with her hand on André's shoulder as at their coming.

The car swung out from the farm along the lane, its headlights picking out the remaining traces of snow in sheltered hollows of the Causse. As it turned on to the road for the descent to Saint-André-sur-Audan, the young woman exclaimed,

"Look, Albert, look at the moon!"

Albert glanced across and stopped the car. The moon rising over the valley was part-hidden by shadow in a cloudless sky.

"Ah, yes, there's an eclipse tonight."

He switched off the engine and they sat awhile in the silence of the night, small in the immensity of the landscape, bewitched by the progressive darkness across the face of the moon.

It did not seem strange to the young woman to be there alone with Albert. She was comfortable in his presence, and confident now. At last the car drove on again and as it dipped into the obscurity of the pine-forests down a series of hairpin bends, she said,

"Albert, may I ask you something?"

"What is it?" He could not look at her because of the nature of the road.

"Why are Philippe and Sylvie against the English language? Not against the English people," she added hastily. "They were very kind to invite me but..."

"Oh, Helen." There was such consolatory warmth in his voice that her eyes involuntarily filled with tears. "It's not true, not altogether true, that they are against English being taught at the College. Yes, maybe Philippe is but it's part of a wider issue. He means no harm. Don't take it personally. He's a kind man but he has his principles. We do not always see eye to eye on many matters. As for Sylvie," he took a deep breath, selecting his words with difficulty, "she is not against English. She is against – what shall I say – losing her son. So is Philippe, but in a different way."

The car emerged from the trees. The lights of Saint-André-sur-Audan could be seen at the bottom of the valley. The moon was no longer visible, not because of the eclipse but because it was too low in the sky to be seen from there.

"Why do you all talk in riddles?" The young woman was exasperated.

"We don't. You cannot expect to understand a whole mentality in two or three weeks."

"I'm sorry, Albert, really. It's just that... Do you know Camus' *The Plague*?"

"Of course."

"Remember Rambert, the journalist from Paris who didn't feel part of Oran, didn't identify with problems there? Not to begin with, anyway."

"I remember."

"Well, I'm here and I want to be part of here. I want to have affection for this place."

"Do you think affection is born of one's will?"

"What I mean is, I like being here, I love the place, but I need to know more to love it more. Albert, you're all so kind to me, but I don't want to live on the surface of things. I don't want to be a foreigner here. There's so much I don't understand."

"Such as?"

"Oh, everything. Take André, for example. I thought I'd got a good rapport with him. Tonight he treated me like a stranger."

"He's an adolescent. They're all moody. Besides, he's usually quiet when his mother is there."

"But even when she – you – fetched the logs, he didn't change." She remembered the look they had exchanged. "Well, not really."

"Do not attribute so much importance to things. Being new here, you haven't yet learned to set them in context. But I think I understand what you are saying. I'll try to help."

"Monique too?"

"Monique too. Which reminds me, she's expecting you for dinner tonight. Okay?"

"Lovely. Thanks, Albert. Thanks for talking."

"My pleasure, Helen."

That night, for the first time, they addressed each other with the familiar *tu* form instead of the more formal *vous*. Albert was showing he understood and she felt already she had moved on to a different plane of existence in Saint-André-sur-Audan. She slept with the comfort of that knowledge as a child sleeps with a much-wanted new toy.

The following day M. Noiret asked to see her in his office. Her immediate reaction was that she had done something wrong or had overlooked something or, worse, had offended. Then she thought that maybe it was bad news: there were problems at home; or what if Chantal wanted to end the exchange and return? Oh no, she couldn't bear to be torn away before her allotted time. She had hardly begun.

As she entered, she saw at once that there was no really bad news.

"Miss Camberley, do come in and sit down. Now, is everything all right?"

"Yes, thank you, unless I have inadvertently caused you problems."

"Ha!" M. Noiret, sitting at his table, lifted both hands in a gesture of exaggerated amazement. "On the contrary, you are as conscientious as Chantal Boileau herself. Speaking of whom, I've had a letter from her. She's also settled in well, but finds the English days rather long. Your system is different over there, I gather."

"Yes, it is, very. I'm glad she's settled in though. I did just wonder if you were going to ask me to leave because she wanted me to come back."

"Heavens, no. Nothing like that. Just tell me how you're getting on."

She talked of her classes, praised the quality of their English and their enthusiasm to learn and mentioned two or three particularly gifted pupils, including André Massaud.

"He'll go far," she concluded.

"I'm afraid he won't," said M. Noiret, leaning his elbows on the table and clasping his hands together. "Chantal Boileau made the mistake of telling his parents he was university material. They said it was far too early to tell, but in any case she wasn't to put ideas into his head. He wasn't going to go to university."

"May I ask why not?"

"From what I can gather, M. Massaud doesn't want his son to leave the district. He fears that if André goes away to university he may not want to return to live here, where they need all the young people they can get to stay. Otherwise the valley will die. You can see for yourself, there are few pupils here already, from quite a wide area. If we have too few pupils, the College will be closed, families will not want to live here. It would be too far for the children to travel. But if local children like André stay and marry, then the life of the village – and hopefully the College – will continue. Do you see?"

Yes, she saw.

"I hope I have not been indiscreet in telling you all this," went on M. Noiret, "especially as I know you are involved with the Massauds through the Rodez family. I think, however, you should be careful about what you say about André's aptitude for English."

"But can we not encourage him to further his studies? It's in his best interests, after all."

"Is it? I really cannot say. He will go into the hotel business with his uncle. I expect it has been arranged already. His English will be useful in his dealings with tourists."

"Can't he have a say in what he wants out of life?"

"Only in so far as it agrees with the family decision. It's quite usual, you know."

This was true. In England also she knew of pupils who preferred to comply with their parents' wishes than to fulfil their own potential. But the reason was usually financial or some other family problem, not the life or death of a community.

After that, she began to see Saint-André-sur-Audan with new eyes. Before, when she had explored the village, she had imagined knights riding through in their quest for the Holy Grail, or ladies in wimples at turret windows, entertained by troubadours singing in the streets below. In the prevailing silence it had been so easy to forget the twentieth century with its vehicles and machines and go back in time amid the medieval walls. Never had she considered the future. "The valley will die." Strong emotive words from the principal. Surely it could not be so. And what difference would one boy's education make? Or more precisely, what difference would his learning of English make?

She searched the village, noting inhabited houses whose shutters were flung wide during the day, where washing draped along the side of a tunnel to dry or was hung out high on ledges and terraces. Indeed, there were few signs of life within the ramparts, though beyond, at newer houses, dogs barked, dodging to and fro behind the garden railings, as she walked by. Most buildings, however, slept the winter away behind firmly closed shutters.

The next time she chanced upon the old priest she asked him how many people lived in the village.

"Maybe about a hundred at the moment. But remember, mademoiselle, it's winter. Most people are away for one reason or another. They'll be back by Easter and then in summer the village is crowded. It's a pity you see it like this with so few inhabitants. You're not too bored, I hope."

"No, no," protested the young woman as if for the first time. "I like the village as it is."

The village as it was: vulnerable, dying.

Chapter Three

At the weekend the Rodez family took her by car along the valley road close to the river and overhung by rocks. At one corner they got out to look across the fast-flowing Audan. All was quiet. On the opposite bank stood a village, the stone houses huddled together under their *lauze* roofs pitched at different heights, the whole at one with the barren landscape, hardly distinguishable against the rock-face.

"There he is, there he is," sang Anne Sophie, the eldest child, pointing. She and Laurence began waving.

"You see that old man walking between the river and the house?" said Monique. "He's the only person who lives in that village in winter now."

"And in summer?"

"The place is full of tourists who have to get there by boat. The houses are second homes or made into flats to rent."

The young woman was strangely troubled to be spying on a human being as one watches an endangered species in its natural habitat.

"What happened to all the others in the village?"

"They died, they moved away, mostly to the towns for work or to be near relatives who had left earlier."

"But that's awful. The poor man." She asked the inevitable question, "Do you think this could ever happen to Saint-André-sur-Audan?"

Monique shrugged. "We believe not, but who knows. There aren't many of us with children in the village, and hardly any newcomers. A policeman and his wife have come to live near us; they might have children... If all the children stay on in the village, then there's hope. And if Albert, as mayor, can do what he wants to do, I think it will survive."

Albert lifted little Nathalie into his arms as if to prove a point: "Our children are our future. But it is up to us to provide for our children so that they can stay. As mayor I have a particular responsibility to the people of Saint-André-sur-Audan. I have to think ahead."

"It's not easy, is it, my darling?" Monique smiled up at her husband. "He comes up against a lot of opposition, especially from those who cling to the past."

"We have every right to be proud of our history and our culture," said Albert. "But circumstances – and values – change. We've got to move with the times and seize today's opportunities. At Saint-André-sur-Audan we have two choices, as I see it. Either we eventually move out like the inhabitants of the village over there, which I don't want to happen, or we make it into a dynamic village that pulses with new life. I see no other alternative, frankly."

"Not everybody sees it that way, though," Monique went on, "even in the family."

"You mean Philippe?" asked the woman.

"That's right. He means well, and he's sincere, but he and others like him slow down any plans for future development."

"Even I would hate to see the village die," said the woman, "and I'm new here."

"In a way," said Albert, "the very fact that you are here erodes what Philippe believes to be the essence of the village. Forgive me, Helen, but do you understand what I mean? People from outside are a threat unless they marry locally and settle. That's his idea, not mine."

The young woman did not comment. Her gaze followed the lone figure in the landscape, the old man who slowly, stiffly, reached a house which took him in, barred him from view and stood with its neighbours like a sentinel, guarding the privacy of its desolation. And there she stood, unprotected, excluded from *the essence of the village*, as if she were to blame for its decline, as if she had brought a fatal disease to the native people.

Albert, Monique and the children were standing close together, complete in their family group, setting her apart. She moved further away, ostensibly to gain a different angle on the valley, in reality showing that yes, she took to heart what Albert was saying: she could not understand the mentality; affection for the place could not be born of one's will, but of one's belonging. Outsiders could not belong.

"My poor Helen." Monique came towards her and took her arm. "My husband is filling your mind with sad thoughts. We're going to show you something which we hope will cheer you up, something for the future, something for everyone, not just local people. We realise the world is a big place and we cannot ignore it in our little valley, Albert has some wonderful plans. Just wait and see."

They drove back to Saint-André-sur-Audan and continued out on the other side for about five hundred metres, turning to the right down a steep track built from the road to where a grassy slope extended to the river's edge. It had oak trees here and there, still decked in their brown leaves.

"Now this," said Albert, waving a hand dismissively around, "is village land. It's used as a simple camp-site in summer. Now where's the future in that? It neither attracts tourists nor creates jobs locally. But just look. The site itself is impressive, isn't it?"

On a bend of the green-blue river, the site commanded views both up- and down-stream and was dominated by crags and cliffs softened by wooded slopes and terraces. Higher still was a thick belt of pines, their dark tops silhouetted against massive outcrops of rock reflecting the pink of the late afternoon sun. The site itself was in shadow and the air was chill.

"The plan is," went on Albert, "to create a huge centre owned by the village. It would be like a large hotel but with every kind of amenity to encourage people to come all year round. Indoor swimming pool, sports hall, cinema, lecture rooms, that sort of thing. In summer, the river is safe here for bathing; we could have a couple of tennis courts, and then there's the usual boating and canoeing which are available in summer anyway. If we can attract the tourists in every season, then that means a lot of work for local people. In the winter months we could even hire it out for conferences, or study groups. With some publicity to begin with we could make it a going concern, I'm absolutely positive. At the moment, we're just playing at tourism. Tourists arrive in summer; they find lodging and food and drink. But we don't actively encourage and exploit tourism for the good of the area. Oh, we put on a little craft exhibition here, a little concert there; we illuminate the bridge and the church on summer nights and we hire out a dozen or so canoes every day. That's not going to have any effect on the economy at all."

Monique chuckled and tapped her husband's arm. "Calm down, my darling, you're not trying to convince your council committee now. I agree with you and so do some others. As for the rest, you will either convince them or they will resign."

But Albert had taken his *élan*. "Just imagine what a difference a centre like this for, say, two hundred people at a time, would make on the village. There'd be jobs for everyone, one way or another. Think of the organisation it would need, the maintenance, not to mention the building of it in the first place, the service staff, the chefs, the suppliers. We could even have activities such as rock-climbing and potholing. There's nothing we couldn't do between us in the village. And you see, the village would own it. It would give this part of the valley a new heart, new life. Do you see?"

Yes, the young woman saw. Albert had ideas to move the village forward into the twenty-first century, whilst safeguarding the integrity of the environment.

"It's very early days yet. We are still at the heated argument stage. I've got most of the younger councillors on my side, those who realise we have to do something before it's too late. The older ones are opposed to encouraging tourism, and so are some of the younger ones, come to that. Take Philippe."

"But he'd gain, wouldn't he?" said the woman, "since he helps the builder."

"Oh yes, financially he would," said Albert, "but it's against his principles. As he said the other night, he's against tourists."

"Because they're outsiders," she concluded. "But everywhere there are tourists, so why not here? Yes, Albert, yes, it's a brilliant idea. When it's built, I'll bring the first group from England."

Albert turned to bestow upon her the full charm of his rare smile.

"If you did that, we would definitely count you as one of us, wouldn't we, Monique?"

"Absolutely. You would merely be in exile while in England."

They all laughed; the children, not understanding but aware of the happiness, laughed too.

"Now back to our little hotel," said Albert, "and we'll let Helen make us all a cup of tea in true English style."

"Aha," she laughed. "You are exploiting outsiders already!"

All the following week she lived contentedly, satisfied with her relationship with the Rodez family, hopeful for the future of the village, at ease with her pupils. She was midway through her stay. The days were lengthening; there were early violets in the square by the church and catkins by the bridge. On sunny afternoons she climbed up the slope to sit on a rock watching the shadow of the Causse opposite gradually covering the village until she grew cold and returned to the warmth of her flat.

Chapter Four

On the Sunday she was driven up to Mas Saint-André as arranged. André ran out to greet them, kissing the family as they emerged from the car and, to her immeasurable delight, running round to kiss her too. Once inside, they were joined by his parents who had been in the kitchen. Out came the inevitable bottles and glasses. There was so much toing and froing of children looking for the cat and animated talk about all the work connected with the killing of the pig that the young woman was not the main object of attention, though her presence was acknowledged. She noticed Sylvie's eyes turn to Albert when he addressed the English mademoiselle as *tu*, but Sylvie made no such concession when she showed them to their seats round the great dining table.

The woman found herself sitting opposite the boy who, hardly glancing at her throughout the meal, preferred to tease his little cousins and help his mother carry the dishes from the kitchen.

"You must forgive my husband," said Sylvie, drawing attention to the pocket knife Philippe was using at table. "He's a peasant."

The woman, aware for a few moments of the clock's regular ticking, finally commented on the excellence of the meal. As promised, the main course, after the green salad and *fricandeau*, the local pâté, was black pudding and pork fillets served with whole apples baked in the oven and sauté potatoes. Philippe was clearly pleased by her compliments as it was, he said, a traditional meal.

"Fortunately," he went on, "some good things don't change with the times. Now take these cheeses, for instance. They're all made in this part of France. That's Cantal, that's Roquefort, made from ewes' milk, and these local cheeses are made from goats' milk."

Next came a glazed apple tart, Sylvie's speciality, it appeared.

"In summer my sister supplies the hotel with fruit tarts and gateaux for the guests' meals," explained Monique.

"Lucky guests," said the young woman and another slice was promptly put on her plate.

"Lucky guests," echoed little Laurence hopefully. Amid the laughter that followed she received her reward.

After coffee, it was agreed that everyone should go for a stroll to a viewpoint at the edge of the Causse, beyond the hamlet of Mas Saint-André. They set off together, with Sylvie telling the young woman the recipe for the apple tart. But as they walked along the narrow lane, Monique went ahead with the children, Sylvie moved up to join her brother-in-law and the English woman found herself with Philippe.

Emboldened by the security of her relationship with the Rodez family, by the temporary nature of her appointment at the College and no doubt to an even greater degree by the oft replenished glasses of wine, her protestations having been half-hearted and ignored, she took command of the conversation.

"Your son is truly gifted in English, you know. He's my best pupil. Doesn't that please you, to know that?"

"You know I'm against English being taught?"

"Yes, you told me. That's not what I asked."

"Okay. Well, to answer your question, mademoiselle, yes, I am pleased my son is a serious pupil. His teacher, Mademoiselle Boileau, thinks he has flair and should continue his studies. And you, too, you are doing a good job for him, I'm not denying that, and André is proud to have a real English teacher. He was so excited before you came."

"And afterwards, was he disillusioned?" She smiled, knowing this not to be so.

"On the contrary, but we don't encourage him. English, you see, could take him away."

"I don't understand."

"English is international; it's a passport to much of the world. But it's not the language of here. Do you know what Occitan is, the local dialect?"

"Yes, I've heard of it."

"Occitan is the language to be taught at the College, not English. It's our language, but if it's not taught now, it will disappear, the language and a whole way of thinking, a life-style. It'll go, it has gone. We were identified by belonging to the whole culture of Occitan, but now it's lost to my generation and to future generations.

No one will be left to teach it. My own son knows only a few phrases my parents taught him but he's learning to speak a language anyone and everyone will speak. It's the death of the area. Nobody cares, nobody has ever cared except us. The people in the north, the people of the cities, to them we are just peasants. My wife, she was joking just now, she is my wife, she belongs here now; I'm not talking about her. I'm talking about the people with power or the people who are arrogant enough to dictate to us because we live in the country, because we have a different accent, because they think we are stupid. But we know, we know about our life, we know about death, we know our land. We care for this part of France but they, the ones in their offices, they know nothing, nothing. They draw a line through our valley on the map and that's that, gone, erased; it's better to have people together, it saves on services, it saves on schools. Let's have everyone the same, all talking the same, all learning the same. Education, they call it, but for what? It sends young people away from their roots, it gives them ideas. But they become lost souls, they're not happy in the world or even elsewhere in France. We fight, we have fought for our country. But those who accept that we're French don't accept that we have our ways too that are different. Just imagine what it would be like if every area of France made the same cheese. Unimaginable, unthinkable. So why take our culture, our language away? It's our identity. It goes with the land, it's our heritage passed on to us by our ancestors. They were poor, our ancestors, but what they have passed on is worth keeping."

"Oh dear," exclaimed Sylvie, looking over her shoulder. "Is my husband on his hobby-horse, mademoiselle? Darling, you can be so boring, you know, to people from outside."

"Not at all, not at all," cried the young woman. She slackened her pace to widen the gap between themselves and those in front. "Please, monsieur... Philippe... please go on. It interests me, truly it does. Do go on."

"Forgive me, mademoiselle... may I call you Helen? I do not wish to bore you or be rude. I bear you no grudge, no grudge at all. I am not against the English, far from it, and you do us honour to eat at our table. No, I speak the truth. It's our own people I argue with and some at least should know better. Decisions are taken, long-term decisions which are wrong, wrong, and they don't see that they are killing the village, killing the valley. They're not doing it deliberately, but the result is the same. There are so few of us now to fight for the area. Once the villages were full, but now... Did you know that the next village down the valley has one inhabitant? One old man? If that can happen there then why not all along the river? Consider Saint-André-sur-Audan. It's deserted in winter. Not a cat, as we say. I exaggerate, but you know what I mean. Empty houses, closed shutters, no cafés. What sort of a village is that?"

Philippe stood for a moment or two to allow the others to move completely out of earshot, then they both resumed their steady pace.

"I suppose Albert has told you about his plans for the village?"

"Yes, last weekend, if you mean the old campsite."

"I do. What do you think?"

"As far as I'm concerned, as an outsider if you like to put it that way, it seems a wonderful idea of providing work and ensuring the future of the village. It's the in-thing, you know, the tourist industry, and the village would be more in control of its own destiny."

"I hear my brother-in-law's words in what you say there," commented Philippe wryly. "He speaks of tourism as if it's God. Everything revolves round it; it becomes our master. Look what happens. Townspeople buy up houses for holiday homes. We hardly see them from September to July. The shopkeepers and café owners come from away to take the profits in summer then off they go to other resorts with a longer season. Neither party has any real interest in the village."

"But Albert's plan is to maintain tourism all the year round," said the woman. "Local people – and their children – will be encouraged to stay."

"It's a false god," continued Philippe. "If we put too much hope in it, it will let us down. It means we all depend on outsiders. It is the prostitution, yes, prostitution of the valley. We debase ourselves. Even if his major project doesn't go ahead, he wants to encourage tourism by offering night-life, discos, concerts by the river. I tell you, that is not in keeping with the area. If tourists want night-life and discos let them go back to the cities where they came from. Why should they expect us to change our life-style so that they needn't change theirs? We humiliate ourselves."

"But, Philippe, what alternative is there?" exclaimed the young woman. "You talk of the past as if it can be brought back. It can't. I'm sorry about the Occitan dialect, truly I am. I'm sorry that people are leaving the valley. But that's the way it is and Albert is doing his best. Even you, with respect, haven't clung entirely to the old ways. You have electricity, television, a car. In the little supermarket in Saint-André-sur-Audan you can buy produce from all over the world. This valley is only part of a whole, which is changing all the time. What would people around here think if children at the College weren't given the same opportunities as those everywhere else? What if they were denied English? They wouldn't be equipped for the future. Don't you realise that in England I teach French? I want my students not just to learn one set of words for another, but to appreciate what goes with the French language in the same way as you talk about Occitan – the way of thinking, the culture, the people, yes, even the food and wine. Aren't you proud of that? And if André does well in English, he's widening his horizons, yes, but he's not turning his back on you or on the area. He can use it to his advantage – for tourism if necessary. Oh, Philippe, I'm sorry, I shouldn't have said that. Forgive me. It is not for me to question your wishes for your son. You are going to think badly of me."

Their eyes met, and once again she was aware of the blueness of his, like André's.

"Oh no, mademoiselle, Helen, no, no. You have listened to me. I have listened to you. We have both been honest with each other. I like that. You disagree with me but I appreciate what you say. My son, you know, is very fond of you. I realise why. You are direct. I am glad he works well for you. I should try to encourage him, you say."

"That's my opinion. By discouraging him in English you are not offering him an alternative. May I ask what you'd like him to do?"

"I want him to stay here. That's the main thing. I suppose what I'd really like is to see him running the farm. But he enjoys working for his uncle, so I expect he'll do what his mother wants, unless I can persuade him otherwise, and join the tourist trade."

"There you are. He stays because of tourism."

"And helps spoil the valley? Or else he leaves to follow the trade elsewhere."

"That's a risk, it's true. All parents face that problem. But if André is as happy at the Hotel de l'Audan as I'm given to believe, then he'll stay. He could end up as the manager of the new complex one day and help the valley survive. What's wrong with that? But without tourism, what could he realistically do? Farming? You know yourself it is no longer viable."

"Not as it is at present. It's as I say, nobody cares. We're left to fight alone. If the will was there we could get the area back to what it was, without relying on tourists."

They were approaching the very edge of the gorge where the others stood waiting, with Albert and Monique holding their children firmly by the hand. As they all peered straight down into the valley below, the young woman immediately recognised the stretch of road and the camp-site she had been shown the previous week. So, Albert's great temple to tourism would scar the landscape after all, not that of Saint-André-sur-Audan but of Mas Saint-André, from this viewpoint. Aware of Philippe watching her, she flashed him a glance which told him she understood: Albert's plan would desecrate what Philippe believed to be his heritage.

"See all those old terraces, Helen?" Philippe was pointing to the lower part of the gorge on both sides, where the slopes, layered, levelled and supported by stone walls, were so much part of the landscape that the young woman had not considered them. "In former times they were full of vines and almond trees."

"It must have been beautiful in spring," she said, "with all the almond blossom."

"Oh yes, but there was a lot of work to do. Vines and almond trees demand a lot of attention. Think of all the people who laboured in the fields." Philippe was again thinking of his ancestors.

They looked down at the barren slopes. Now there was no one to tend the vineyards, to till the earth, to tread where their forefathers had trodden; what lives had been centred on those terraces, what anxieties had been all-important in their building and maintenance, what joys had echoed in laughter from field to field? A hotel complex was indeed a poor substitute for what had gone before, but the past was irretrievably lost as the bare terraces showed.

When the group set off again the young woman found herself once again with Philippe, behind Albert and Sylvie, only this time they were joined by André. They began to talk about the days when all along the valley the terraces were green with vines.

"But Philippe," said the young woman, "I thought that vine-growing was big business now. It's all chemicals and machines and vast lands."

"We could form co-operatives as they do elsewhere. Yes, it could work. But the will isn't there, you see. People want money; local people have been lured into tourism. I tell you, mademoiselle, it's not the answer."

Sylvie had stopped and called out, "Come along, André, my darling, don't dawdle. You'll be like your father, always left behind."

"I'm listening to the conversation," said André.

"What you're listening to you've heard umpteen times before. Do come on, my son. I've something to say to you."

André ran off to join his mother and uncle.

"You see my son?" Philippe went on. "Lads not much older than him, still in their teens, went off from here to the war in 1914 until 1918. All the boys, all the young men, all the fathers and husbands and brothers and sons, they all left this valley. They'd never been out of their villages, they were country people, no not peasants, men who lived here with fierce pride for their land, for their families, men who pruned their vines and worked the soil. And what happens? One day they are taken off to fight for their country. They go up north where France is a foreign country to them – it's cold, it's wet, it's flat. And the generals say, 'They're only peasants from nowhere; put the buggers at the front, let them get killed, they're not important; they don't even talk like us, stupid peasants.' And they're put in the front lines because these men, they're not stupid, but they're brave, they're strong, they won't chicken out and they die, all of them, they die in the mud of the north, far from their beloved valley, every man and boy of them, they die. They're honoured, yes, they're honoured all right: they became mere lists of names carved in stone. In our villages, have you seen all our war memorials, all our monuments to the dead? You have them in England, yes? But here, look at the names, all the same families. Look at the village and count: how many houses are there? how many names are there? So no one came back, no one came to care for the vineyards. The women, they tried, in honour of their menfolk, but they too were uncared for, deserted. And the children, they grew up and tried to carry on. But it was too late. The rhythm of the years was broken. It was the end, the beginning of the end. And yes, you're right. There was competition, they couldn't afford the machines, they couldn't afford to work the land. They had to look elsewhere. They went to the towns; there was work there. And still they go. And now here we are."

The young woman looked around, then realised he was still talking about the fate of the valley. He mistook her movement for boredom and apologised.

"My wife tells me I talk too much about the past. But how can we go forward without knowing where we are and where we've been? Some people scorn the past, but then they make mistakes for the future. That's what I think, anyway. Am I such an idealist, do you find?"

"Maybe. Sometimes you have to adapt to changed circumstances, you know."

They walked on in silence towards the farmhouse. Then Philippe said, "Perhaps that's what they were told when they went to war."

But when she looked at him, there was only kindness in the blueness of his eyes and she felt at one with him. As they approached the house, she said, "Thanks for sharing with me, Philippe. I'm a foreigner but I want a sense of belonging here. Although you have made me realise I'm not one of you, not part of the valley, you've given me deeper understanding. I can never be a mere tourist admiring the views and old buildings. I can see the heart within. You have shown me what visitors don't see."

"I'm glad, Helen. I still stand by my principles, but you're the only English person I know and you have shown me the heart behind the English language, too. We shall meet again before you go back to England, I hope."

They did indeed meet, for reasons unforeseen, which brought principles and goodwill into conflict.

Chapter Five

André stayed behind after an English lesson one day to ask if he could talk some things over. Thinking it concerned work that had just been done in class, the young woman sat down and opened her book. The boy, however, said no, it was not the work, but he wanted to see her sometime soon. He insisted, his eyes searching hers, demanding an answer with all the beseeching guile and earnestness of his youth. She was glad, glad that he had wanted to be with her, but something about the intensity of his manner made her apprehensive. She agreed to see him that day, before afternoon school.

He was already waiting there by the door of her classroom when she arrived. They sat by a poster of Piccadilly Circus where red double-decker buses stood as still as the statue of Eros.

"Well?"

"You'll be going home soon, won't you, back to England?"

"Not yet. I've another three weeks here."

"That's soon, though. And then Mademoiselle Boileau comes back?"

"She'll be back a day or two before I leave, I think. Why?"

The boy paused, looked down at the table then straight at the young woman.

"Take me to England. I want to go with you."

"André!"

"I want to go."

"André! You don't know what you're saying. You're not serious."

"I am, I am. Don't go without me. Don't leave me." He put his arms out across the table to her in a dramatic gesture.

"André!"

She had sat back on her chair in an attempt to distance herself, but relaxing she leaned forward and put her hands across the sleeves of his pullover.

"André, listen. You know what you're asking is impossible. You can't really mean it. What on earth made you think of such a thing?"

The boy looked away as his eyes filled with tears. He shrugged. To speak would be to break down, she saw that.

"Look, André. You're good at English and I'm pleased with you. You were the first pupil I met. Do you remember when I arrived and you prepared my breakfast?"

He nodded, averting his eyes.

"But I've got to go back to England and you've got to stay here. You're very lucky to belong to this area, you know. You should be proud of it."

Still the boy, silent, did not look at her.

"I don't expect for a minute your parents know. What were you thinking of?"

Receiving no answer she said, "Look, when I get home I'll try to get penfriends for your class and for you in particular. All right? But I'm not going yet. Don't remind me of going back. I don't want to think about it. Now what's your next lesson? It's nearly time."

Lifting her hands from his sleeves, she rose. He scraped his chair back and getting up made for the door, wearing all the indignity of his humiliation across his shoulders.

"André."

He stopped and half-turned.

"Thanks for wanting to go with me to England. I appreciate that but, well, you know it's impracticable."

"If you say so."

He looked at her, his eyes so full of hurt that she wanted to hold him, comfort him, stroke his dark hair and reassure him it was all right, she understood.

But instead she heard herself saying, "Off you go then. I'll see you in class tomorrow."

He closed the door behind him, leaving her alone amid the maps and pictures. A tea-towel of Anne Hathaway's cottage was pinned between the posters of a beefeater and the Loch Ness monster. What did the boy really understand of Britain? It was all so superficial, so far away, so foreign, was it a dreamland of opportunity and happiness for the boy torn between the philosophies of his father and uncle in a dying valley? Or did he just want to be with her?

Later in the cosy solitude of her flat, reflecting on the conversation, she wondered if she had been too harsh, too negative. Many a pupil of his age wanted to travel abroad; it was a natural extension of their studies. She had contacts with whom he could stay to be with other children. He could even stay with her, in the little spare room of her mid-terrace house. Returning with her in February would be out of the question, of course, but if summer were proposed, his keenness would be put to the test in the delay. Should the visit go ahead, he could attend her English school after term had finished in France. As the evening wore on, she convinced herself of the possibility, of the viability, of the desirability of such a visit, with the anticipated pleasure of having the boy's company, improving his English, widening his experience.

But the boy's parents would surely oppose any suggestion that their son should so much as leave the valley, considering it nothing short of treason by the infiltrator in their midst, a betrayal of their trust; yet one could not ignore the boy's cry for help. By the time she went to sleep she had made up her mind: the boy would be with her in England.

She mentioned the idea in confidence when she next saw Monique, without referring to the conversation with André. It was enough for his aunt to know that the opportunity was there for him to visit England.

"We saw this coming, Albert and I," was Monique's response. "He was so excited about having you as a teacher, especially as you'd be spending so much time with us, as part of the family. I expect he has said something to you, yes? That's our André. He has an idea, he wants something and he goes all out to get it. Last year, out of the blue, he told us he wanted to spend the summer holidays here, helping in the hotel. It caused quite an upset, I can tell you, especially with his father, who didn't approve. My sister wasn't happy to see him here with me instead of in Mas Saint-André, so she spent a lot of time here, too. It worked out all right in the end, but..."

"Even that's different from going all the way to England. I suppose the idea would meet with disapproval."

"His parents wouldn't let him go, I'm sure."

"That's what I thought."

"There's no harm in asking. Go and put it to them. Albert could drive you up to Mas Saint-André one day. My husband and I wouldn't object, of course, to André's going to England, especially if it meant being where you live. He wouldn't be with strangers. He'd soon be back helping us here in the hotel. But I think it would help him to grow up, to get away from the family for a while. My sister doesn't always appear to realise he's not her little boy any more. She sometimes treats him as if he's the age of my girls. Philippe wanted to make a man of his son, it's true, but for him that means a man of the land. He'd like André to help him lead a revival of the old life-style in the area. At least Sylvie sees now he has a future with us, in tourism."

"Monique, what would happen if André did so well at school he wanted to go to university?"

"Knowing André, I suppose he would probably end up doing what he wanted, but I can't see much support from his parents, quite frankly. Besides, he's got everything he needs here. There's no pot of gold at the end of the rainbow, so why go great distances to look for it? His roots are here with his family and friends. His future will be here, especially if Albert manages to persuade the village – and the authorities for a grant – to go ahead with the new hotel scheme. Then André's English could be very useful. So there's no point in going to university, is there?"

"But you've nothing against his going to England?"

"For a couple of weeks? Not at all. Mind you, I'm not his mother. You'd better wait and see what his parents say."

Despite himself, André was still a good pupil. Since his request had been turned down, he had begun by appearing withdrawn, sullen almost, unwilling to contribute, fiddling with his watch or fixing his gaze on a nearby poster. The young woman had let him be, appearing not to notice by giving her attention elsewhere. It worked. The boy could not bear to be ignored and eventually sought her help in a written exercise. She, close to him, gently explained, pretending the pretext was genuine and smiled at him before moving on, while his eyes tried to delay her.

She did not let him know of her idea for summer but the thought of asking permission of his parents without the prior knowledge of his reaction disturbed her inwardly to such an extent that she was gripped by apprehension whenever it came to mind. It would have been easy to abandon the idea, let the matter rest. He was after all only a pupil, to whom she had no obligation; moreover, anything that influenced him to question his father's views on the future or to distance himself from his mother would be seen as a deliberate attempt to undermine their authority. Then she saw the narrowness of the world in which in which he was imprisoned and realised she could offer to show him beyond. After that, it would be up to him.

The opportunity to speak to his parents came, not by a drive up to the Causse with Albert, but one Wednesday afternoon when they met by chance at the butcher's. In truth, it was not so much by chance as it appeared for the young woman, sitting on the slope above the College, had noticed a car coming down from the Causse and on returning to her flat some minutes later had watched for it to go down the hill below her living-room window. She had spotted André in the back.

Running down through the maze of alleys she had seen Sylvie and Philippe emerge from the hotel car-park, no doubt leaving André with Monique and family. She had strolled into the butcher's shortly after they had entered.

They greeted her, immediately lapsing into the familiar *tu* form to ask how she was and if she was looking forward to returning to England. It was the perfect time to ask if they would join her at her flat for a cup of English tea. They agreed and, after they had bought their steak and she some pâté, together they went through the tunnel leading up into the old village and climbed the steep cobbled way to the College.

"You've got a nice place here," commented Sylvie, looking round the flat and admiring the view from the window.

"I'll be sorry to leave it," said the young woman, pouring water into a saucepan and putting it on the electric ring. "It's been ideal, and so handy for work. Do you know what I really like about this place? My daily ritual of opening and closing the shutters."

The other two looked puzzled.

"You see, in Britain we don't have shutters."

"No shutters?" cried Sylvie, as shocked as if she'd told them the British still lived in caves. "I could never live in a place without shutters. Why don't you have them?"

"We just don't," replied the English woman. "For us, that's normal. We do have curtains though, so that people can't see in if the light is on."

"Even so, it's not the same."

"As for me," said Philippe, "I wouldn't like all the rain and fog you have in England."

"That's a bit of a myth, you know. The weather's not so bad, not usually. You should come over one day and see."

"No thanks. We like our French ways too much," said Sylvie. "We've been told that the food isn't good in England. Everything is boiled, you overcook your meat, you have mint sauce and your bread isn't crusty."

The woman smiled. "It's not all bad, you know." She glanced at the water in the pan. It was not yet boiling.

"I was wondering," she said slowly. "I was wondering if maybe your son would like to visit me in summer."

"In England?" Sylvie looked across at her sharply and she felt Philippe's eyes on her too.

"Yes," she said gaily, as if it did not matter particularly to her. "It's only an idea. He's keen on the subject and I thought he might like to..."

"I sincerely hope you've not already invited him," said Sylvie.

"Oh no," she continued in her nonchalant way.

"That's just as well. I don't know what you had in mind, but he's far too young to go away from home, isn't he, darling?"

"It might be..." said Philippe, measuring his words, "It might help him grow up, to get right away while he's still young. Then he'll not feel we've been holding him back and he'll choose to stay here later on."

The young woman recognised Monique's words. It looked as though she had had a quiet word with her brother-in-law.

"Is that really my husband talking, you who are so against, have always been against, English? Don't joke, Philippe; don't trifle with your son's life."

The saucepan was boiling. The young woman removed it from the ring and dropped a tea bag into the water.

"At home we use a kettle and a teapot," she said, "but I didn't bring them with me, so I do it the French way."

Her words went unheeded.

"I am against the teaching of English instead of Occitan. I'm not against Helen. If my son wishes to visit her, I'm sure he would be well looked after."

"But you're mad! Helen lives abroad, not in Pradoux, you know. Do you really want to see your son, my son, go out of the country, you who don't want him to leave Mas Saint-André? Don't be so ridiculous. No, Helen, my son will not be visiting you. We shall be happy to see you back here one day, though."

The young woman poured out the tea.

"Darling," said Philippe, "we could at least thank Helen for considering André."

"I have friends with children of André's age," the young woman persisted, realising she was losing. "He could have stayed with them, or with me. I thought he just might have liked to see the country he'd been learning about. He'd be very welcome, and I'd take good care of him."

"No, no, it's out of the question. My husband and I are grateful to you for the suggestion. André's too young. He's never left home before, except to be with my sister. And what about the journey? All that way alone? No, no, no. Darling, I'm beginning to see why you wanted Occitan taught after all. If I'd thought that learning English would mean going to England..."

"Oh please don't worry. It was only an idea. I meant well." The words came easily, belying her disappointment.

Philippe looked across at her. "It was really kind of you anyway."

Their tea consumed, they sauntered amicably down to the hotel, towards the sound of the river. "I'm not ready to leave yet," said the young woman. If André did not come in summer, her departure would close the shutters on her time in the village with no chink of light. "I like being here."

"Better than England?" asked Philippe.

"Different. I suppose once I'm back I shall pick up my old life again. It's a pity to leave my life here behind, though."

Had André become a symbol of that life?

In the hotel, on the floor of the living-room the children were kneeling, fitting the pieces of a jigsaw puzzle together. Sylvie went across to them and ruffled André's hair.

"Hello, my son. We have just had a cup of tea with your English teacher."

The boy, moving away, looked directly at the young woman, who gave the slightest shake of the head. She had not betrayed his trust.

"That's interesting," Monique said, putting a pile of clothes on a chair by the ironing board set up in one corner. "We've just been having a chat, my nephew and I, haven't we, André?" The meaningful look she cast at the boy was lost on none of the adults.

"I do hope you have not been putting ideas into his head," said Sylvie, her face haughty and set.

"Oh, we were just talking about this and that and we started talking about summer."

"If you want him to work again at the hotel, I have no objection at all," put in Sylvie rather too hastily. "And this year, neither has my husband, have you, darling?"

Philippe shrugged and turned his palms uppermost. "Everybody has ideas for my son, it appears. Nobody in the family listens to me any more. Is he going to be treated the same? André, what do you want to do?"

"I'd like to be at the hotel."

"There you are," cried Sylvie at once, triumphantly. "You said the right thing, my son."

"He hasn't finished yet, have you André?" Monique thumped the iron down on the back of a blouse the young woman recognised as hers. The sleeves hung limp and lifeless from either side of the board.

"I'll do that," she said, meaning it, but Monique dismissed the offer and the interruption.

"André, go on."

"He needn't bother. It's about England, isn't it? You want to go to England? But it's impossible, my darling. It's too far."

"It would only be for a fortnight or so," said the boy, trying to be defiant, but failing to meet his mother's eyes.

"And have you been invited? Has mademoiselle asked you?"

"It was my idea, but Auntie Monique says..."

"So what have you been saying to my son?" Sylvie turned on her sister.

"It's my fault," put in the English woman. "I mentioned to Monique a few days ago that he might like to visit me in summer – the suggestion I put to you just now."

"And you, Monique, told my son. Thank you very much! So you have been putting ideas into his head, as I feared."

"Darling," said Philippe, "let the boy speak, for goodness sake. André?"

Reluctantly, the boy answered. "If you must know, I asked mademoiselle if I could go back with her to England when Mademoiselle Boileau returns. She said I couldn't. Then Auntie Monique suggested summer instead. That's all."

"And you want to go, I suppose?" said his father.

"Yes, I do. But that doesn't mean I don't like living here. You know that, don't you?"

"Yes, my son, I know."

"Oh, Philippe, you're impossible," exclaimed Sylvie. "Don't encourage him. How can the boy possibly go to England on his own? The answer is no. How many more times do I have to repeat myself? Now come along, André, Philippe. Let's hear no more nonsense."

She kissed her nieces and her sister. Her gait proving her command of the situation, she walked out, leaving Philippe and André to say their farewells. André went and offered his face to the young woman who kissed him readily and heard a quiet "Thank you for the invitation" in her ear. Her relationship with the boy had been fully restored.

Chapter Six

The days accelerated as the time of her departure drew near. The newness which had slowed down her first few weeks had given way to contented, measured routine, but now a series of "lasts" quickened the process, inexorably bringing her closer to the date entered on her *couchette* reservation for the night-train to Paris. These were the last letters written home, these the last tests marked, this the last week before Chantal's return, this the last weekend. She felt the wedge easing between herself and the village. Was she leaving, or was the village withdrawing? Whatever it was, she was slipping away faster and faster, out of control.

On the last Sunday, she managed to hold on to the afternoon by attending a Bingo session in the village hall. The room was packed; chairs, with their backs pressed against each other, were grouped around tables. Everyone was there: M. Noiret, since the proceeds were to go to the College, other teachers and their families, the priest she occasionally met in the alleys of the village, children, a babe in arms, everyone had come to this social gathering.

Albert explained to her that many of the people she failed to recognise had come down from the Causses on either side of the gorge. They had weather-beaten faces, lined, carved by experience, with eyes too shrewd, too jealous of their privacy to cast a glance at the English woman staring at them. These were the people, farming folk, who thought like Philippe, who saw the valley with the eyes of the past, who spurned the garish superficiality of tourism. The land was theirs; they had laboured for it with fierce pride, they had fashioned it but it in turn had fashioned them. They would not yield lightly to the demands of the outsider. Some of them, she knew, had been part of the Resistance during the Second World War to repel the Nazis. Now the invasion was insidious; there were more collaborators, people like Albert who as elected mayor was leading his village to triumph or disaster according to which side one was on. But this time there was no glory for those who fought for the integrity of the area, no monuments or medals for Philippe and these folk from the Causses. There was only scorn for their obstinate tenacity or maybe a little pity for those whose lands would die with them, the younger generation having left for the cities or joined forces with the enemy. But the English woman saw the gnarled, rough hands which worked in vain but which worked nevertheless and her admiration grew for these people, for Philippe, who would honour their ancestors to the end, with neither surrender nor compromise.

It was with difficulty that she heard the explanations of the butcher's wife beside her amid the hubbub of voices and scraping of chairs. The air was full of smoke from cigarettes and pipes and full too of an excitement she had not experienced since she had been in France. Attention was drawn to the prizes and a roar of appreciation went up. There were great boxes of groceries, bottles of wine, rabbits, sausages and the main prize, the pig's head.

"I would like to win that," said the young woman to the butcher, "just to be able to tell friends at home."

She did not win, however. In the hushed room (the eventual hush following many shouts for quiet and knocking on tables) M. Noiret called out the numbers and their identifying label: *"Numéro treize, ma sœur Thérèse"*. People around her were calling *"Quine"* and *"Superquine"* and after having had their numbers checked, pushed by, collected their trophy and returned, holding it aloft with all the smugness of success. André squeezed past to receive a box of groceries. Beaming, he took it back to his parents' table where they admired the spoils item by item, a tin of peas, a packet of biscuits, a bottle of cordial as if they were handling treasure trove.

So these were local values: being together, breathing the same smoky air, exchanging news and views across the bingo cards, friendly rivalry, vying with each other for the coveted prizes, success depending on luck as the only criterion. It was right that she did not win, that an outsider did not take away their moment of glory. She saw the pig's head won by an old woman from the Causse who was overcome by being the sudden centre of attention and who kept repeating "I would never have believed it, never in my life" long after the game was over and people began to leave.

Outside in the road engines revved and there was much shunting and reversing before the cars drove away amid farewells and waving.

Small groups of people lingered awhile, talking animatedly, then they too piled into cars and headed up to the Causses. For several minutes the noise of the engines could be heard across the valley as the vehicles wound their way up the rugged sides, then they could just be seen climbing slowly ever upward until they eventually disappeared between the pine trees on the higher slopes. Only the Audan could be heard again.

Albert, emerging from the hall with M. Noiret, locked the door and walked back to the hotel with his family and their English guest who would be spending her last night in her bedroom overlooking the river. She lay awake listening to the sound of the water, trying to store it in her memory, recalling the first time she had slept there, promising herself there would be other times when she would return and claim this room, these sounds as hers.

The next morning, early, she went downstairs to the smell of coffee and shortly afterwards walked up the hill to the College, conscious of the smell of newly baked bread as she passed the baker's and of the wood-smoke hanging in the village. All this she would remember and much, much more. In the afternoon she took her camera and tried to capture views and sights familiar to her: an old doorway, a cobbled alley with an old pump, a flight of steps leading up through a tunnel, the bridge. She gripped the edge of the parapet to the bridge, feeling its solid strength, she brushed her hands across the overhanging bough of catkins by the water's edge, chose a small smooth stone to put in her pocket, looked up at the Causse and saw the road which would take her not to Mas Saint-André which was hidden from view but beyond, to the railway station, to the north, to home.

Consciousness of still being there, standing in the valley, was a contentment all of its own. She breathed the still air; she lived, she understood. The essence of the village she had tried so hard to capture may not be hers for the taking but she recognised its ageing face, heard its slow pulse and felt its gnarled hand on her shoulder. No ordinary tourist could ever see as she saw, feel as she felt. The valley must always have had travellers, always offered accommodation to those passing through. She, however, had tarried, by invitation, to work alongside its people, to educate their children. Even those, like Philippe, who were against what she taught, had treated her kindly; she herself was not seen as some latter-day pied piper who had come to lure the children away from their homes. But what of André? His mother had refused on his behalf when a visit to England had been suggested but since the idea had been originally André's there may now be conflict between mother and son. Then the young woman recalled the bingo session and André's face as he revealed the contents of his box of groceries to his parents. No, his heart had been restored to his home, ideas of seeing her in England forgotten. Regret had no reason to gnaw at her when she thought of it.

During the last days at the College she savoured each moment of each lesson, praised the pupils, joked with them, taught them songs which they sang with gusto. They in turn wrote out their addresses for her to find penfriends for them, brought her gifts and bunches of violets and handmade cards.

It was just after lunch on the Thursday, the day before her departure, that a shout went up from the children playing in the yard. The few teachers who were finishing their coffee in the sudden calm of the dining-hall after the pupils had left, peered out of the window and saw a figure surrounded by excited youngsters.

"It's Chantal Boileau! She's home!"

They left the table to go and greet the newcomer. The English woman hung back, suddenly superfluous as Chantal was welcomed, kissed, drawn into the dining hall. The chef, hearing the commotion, came out of the kitchen and offered a late meal which was accepted.

It was then that Chantal noticed the English woman and she fell on her, kissing her on both cheeks, claiming she felt she knew her so well after teaching her pupils and being with her colleagues; she hoped Helen's time in Saint-André-sur-Audan had been as happy. It was arranged that Chantal would go to the flat that afternoon as they had so much to talk about, then Chantal gave herself over to her own colleagues while she ate the meal the chef had put before her with obvious delight.

"Oh, green salad! Am I glad to see salad again! And more bread, please. I never want to see sliced bread again. Now tell me, what's the news since I've been away?"

The English woman excused herself from the table; she still had a lot of packing to do, and she needed to clean the flat, she said. As she walked out into the yard some of the children ran up to her.

"Did you see Mademoiselle Boileau? She's our English teacher. She says she liked England very much but she's glad to be back."

Already, unknowingly, they were rejecting her. Her time here was over. She belonged elsewhere.

The children moved away, gathering by the dining-hall window. One or two began to sing and others joined in, wanting to attract Mademoiselle Boileau's attention by their rendering of *What shall we do with a drunken sailor?*

M. Noiret loomed up at the window, dispersing the excited children.

"Mademoiselle?"

By the edge of the yard the English woman turned and realised André had run back to her.

"You must be pleased to see your teacher back again," she said hurriedly. "I am sure she'll be happy to teach you all again."

"Yes, I'm glad to see her again," said the boy, "but I want you to..." He stopped, unable to continue.

"But you want me to stay as well? I know. I'd like to stay too, but I have pupils in England now without a teacher. I've got to go back to them."

"Tomorrow?"

"Tomorrow."

"May I come with you as far as the station?"

"You must ask your parents and your uncle. I've so much luggage there may not be room in the car!"

"It's because of all the presents you've been given."

"Yes, that's right. Now, don't you go getting any ideas about jumping on the train, will you?"

"No, don't worry. But I want to see you in the summer."

"André, your mother said you couldn't."

"My father didn't say no, did he? And you didn't. That's a vote of two to one. Three to one if I'm included."

She had not the heart to deny him a dream. "We'll see," she said.

Within the hour Chantal knocked at the flat door. Despite her overnight journey, she was vivacious, enthusiastic, chattering on about her life in England, laughing, confident. She wanted to know how her own pupils had got on and was pleased to hear good reports.

"Life is calmer here, isn't it?" she said. "I really loved every minute of my time in England but I can't understand why English teachers put up with all they have to do. It seems to me a lot of time is wasted doing things other than teaching. Why don't you have different people to do the duties and cover-lessons?"

"You mean like your surveillants? I only wish we could have people like that. But it's not our system. Mind you, we do have a choice as to where we teach and you don't, not at first, anyway. There's good and bad in both systems."

The conversation turned to her weekends at the hotel and, inevitably, to the Massaud family.

"How did you get on with André?"

"Oh, he's wonderful. The quality of his English is very good."

"Yes, he's gifted. I clashed with his parents once by suggesting he could go on to university to read English."

"So M. Noiret said. Isn't it sad? His parents will force him to stay here but they disagree as to what he should do."

"Oh, M. Massaud has given you the Occitan and anti-tourism argument, has he? It's a lost cause, poor man."

"Actually, I found what he said very interesting. He made it quite clear he didn't approve of English, but he treated me with kindness and courtesy. I like him. And do you know, he wasn't against his son's going to England."

"André? Going to England? How come?"

The situation having been explained, and regret expressed that André could not in fact go to England in summer, making the journey alone, Chantal said,

"He can go with me. I'm off to Carlisle for a couple of weeks in July. I'd love to call in to see you, anyway. What are you doing now? Just packing? Come on, let's go and see André's parents now."

"What, now?"

"No time like the present. Come on!"

The English woman had forgotten how to rush. Chantal, on the other hand, newly arrived from her life in England, had not; she had her locking the door, running down the steps and into the little Renault which leaped forward, scattering the wayside pebbles, before the passenger had had time to secure the seat-belt.

The car roared out of the village, up to the first hairpin bend. Chantal directed the car straight at the cliff edge, turning the wheel abruptly at the last moment; the car screeched round to head up the slope to the next corner. The English woman gripped the side of her seat, pressing down her right foot in vain and not daring to look out of the window at the sheer drop she knew to be there. They swung round corner after corner until at long last they were protected on either side by the pine forest from which they eventually emerged on top of the Causse.

They drove towards Mas Saint-André. At the farm, Chantal said, "Leave this to me. I'm André's teacher."

Gladly, reeling from the effects of the journey, the other agreed.

Philippe answered the door, showing no surprise, and invited them in. His wife was out, he said, shopping in Pradoux, but he hoped they would accept his offer of a drink. He welcomed Chantal back to France, asked if everything had gone well for her and if she had enjoyed her stay. Chantal enthused, praising the friendliness of the English, claiming she had eaten well and would miss the life-style of the past few weeks. She wanted, she said, to start up closer links between her pupils in Saint-André-sur-Audan and those in England. Since Monsieur's son was her brightest pupil, she had a proposition to make.

Philippe looked across at the English woman who smiled innocently, thus distancing herself from any suggestion to be put to him.

"I understand", said Chantal, "that you and your wife don't want André to go to England in summer because of his having to travel alone. I'd like you to know that he could travel with me in July, there and back. I'd be pleased to have his company. So, could he go then?"

"I must speak with my wife," said Philippe. "Sylvie doesn't want André to go, but there would be nothing to fear if he went with you and stayed with Helen. I know my son wants to go and I think it would do him good. You see, mademoiselle, I am a reasonable man after all. I have a reputation, I think, for being old-fashioned, for wanting my son to stay here and not go away to study. But if he wants to have a little holiday in England, I shall not say no. I shall do my best to persuade my wife."

The English woman could only speculate as to Sylvie's reaction to the knowledge that her argument had been defeated. There was satisfaction in this defeat, in André's rejection of his mother's wishes, in her annoyance, maybe jealousy.

"Well, that was easy," commented Chantal as the car nose-dived at speed down the road to the valley. "I'm glad Madame Massaud wasn't there, though. She's not a woman to be crossed, especially where her son is concerned."

"I hope we've done the right thing," said the English woman, suddenly anxious at the thought of the responsibility of caring for another's son.

"Absolutely. It'll be an education for the whole family. I'll let you know when to expect us."

Nevertheless, she was ill at ease throughout the rest of the day. She spent her time removing all trace of her two months in the flat, emptying the contents of the wardrobe and cupboards to pack into her suitcases, and sweeping and washing the floors as though covering her tracks. Soon there would be no visible sign that she had ever been in the valley. Her toiling had not fashioned the landscape, as previous generations had built the terraces; but at best it had served to fashion minds, to widen horizons and break down barriers. They trusted her, Albert, Monique, Philippe, André – but what of Sylvie? She would now be aware of the afternoon visitors to the farm.

It was definitely time to leave Saint-André-sur-Audan. To belong, as in her naïveté she had wanted earlier, meant an involvement, with all the resentments and rivalries and bad feelings engendered by close relationships. She was not prepared to fight alone for a place amid people who had so much to guard against intruders. They had treated her very well, had been hospitable and courteous simply because she was different, she was Chantal's replacement and she was not staying long. That was the truth of the matter and in the end it suited her. If Sylvie refused Chantal's offer of accompanying André to England, the break would be complete. Maybe, she persuaded herself, that would be better. What was the child to her, anyway? She sat in the bare living-room. Even the flat had rejected her now, ready to be reclaimed by Chantal again the following week. Leaving would not be difficult.

Goodbyes were said the following day at the College with no sadness, as if long-rehearsed and staged for a public performance. Her hand was shaken many times without her being aware of the physical contact. She took a last look round the empty class-room which had never been hers, but Chantal's all along. She listened to the voices of that room, saw her self-consciousness as she stood for the first time in front of her, no Chantal's, class, saw the bright faces of the pupils, saw André. She closed the door and walked away.

It was when Albert arrived with the car to take her, with all her luggage, back to the hotel for her final dinner that unease returned, like a cogwheel turning with each passing second. And the empty, emotionless state she had been in all day, which she had put down to self-control, gave way to an inner panic as she locked the door to the flat and followed Albert down the steps.

"So," said Albert, as they drove off down the hill, on the road below the little window she had looked out of so frequently. "This is it. The time has gone very quickly, hasn't it?"

"Oh yes, too quickly."

They drove into the hotel car-park, but instead of walking straight into the hotel they went and leaned over the river wall. Fed by recent rains in the mountains, the Audan was in full flow, swirling violently against the rocks before sliding smooth and deep under the span of the bridge.

"Good luck with your venture, Albert," the young woman said at last. "I hope your council agrees to your plans."

"They know the alternative. At least the village would be in control and would benefit both from the work and the profit. But you know that."

She looked beyond the river to the terraces, bleak in the winter shadow with no hope of spring almond blossom.

"Poor Philippe," she said. "I do understand how he feels, but I believe in what you are doing."

"Oh, in time he may change his mind. He has to think of the future in realistic terms, for his son's sake."

They entered the hotel where not only Monique and the girls were waiting for them, but also the three Massauds. The cog-wheel within her turned but her face managed a smile.

"Not too sad to be leaving, then?" asked Sylvie, commanding the situation immediately.

"I'm okay."

"I hope you're hungry," said Monique, bidding her to sit down and pushing a platter of hors d'oeuvre across the table at her.

"Yes, eat well tonight," said Albert. "It'll be your last good meal until you come back to France!"

She laughed. Philippe filled her glass: "The last wine!"

The whole family was attentive, teasing, warm. No one, however, told her what she wanted to know; André's face was inscrutable, as was Sylvie's. The salad bowl was passed round, then the chicken casserole smelling deliciously of thyme, though she ate without appetite. She took a mere spoonful of peas for the vegetable course, amusing the children by demonstrating the English way of eating them on the back of the fork; then she cut for herself a small portion of Cantal cheese. After one of Sylvie's tarts was brought out, served and eaten, the children got down from the table while the adults lingered over their coffee.

Monique looked at her watch. "Goodness, we'd better soon leave!" She scooped up Nathalie and went upstairs, followed by Laurence and Anne Sophie. Almost at once the girls returned to kiss the English woman goodbye, then to kiss the others.

"Off you go. I'm coming up," said Sylvie, then turned to explain: "It appears I'm baby-sitting as Monique would like to go to the station with you, so I'd better go up and get the children ready for bed. Oh, and André will go to Pradoux with his aunt and uncle as well, won't you, my darling? So, mademoiselle, I have to say goodbye now." She came and held out her hand.

The young woman took it. "Goodbye. I hope we meet again, either here or in England."

"Not in England, that's for sure, but in France, why not?"

"I'll see you in England," put in André, "in the summer."

"He says that now, because I have had to agree," said Sylvie in a low voice, almost a mutter, "but he will forget in the summer. I know my son. Other ideas will attract him, like working here, for instance. Well then, goodbye. Have a good journey."

"Are you ready, Helen?" asked Albert.

"Are you coming, Philippe?" she asked in turn.

"No, no. I'm staying here with my wife." He came and stood before her. "Goodbye, Helen. I am very pleased to have met you. I hope we meet again."

"Goodbye, Philippe, and good luck. Thanks for everything." She looked at him, straight at his blue eyes, willing him to kiss her on both cheeks, in true French style. He shook her hand, seemingly unaware of her acute disappointment in such an incomplete farewell.

Monique dashed downstairs. The young woman found herself walking out of the hotel and sitting at the front of the car next to Albert. As the car climbed out of the village, Monique said,

"If you turn round now you'll have your last glimpse of Saint-André-sur-Audan."

She did not have the courage to do so but said, "Sometimes it's best not to look back."

At the station, the train arrived in the darkness with its surge of noise as the locomotive passed and with the silent carriages sliding by and coming to a halt. André ran along the platform to find the right one. Cases and bags were heaved in by Albert's strong arms as Monique kissed her goodbye. Albert turned as if to shake her hand but he too brought her close and kissed her. André kissed her, then she was clambering up the steps, the door was slammed to and she had a moment to see the three faces looking at her before the train moved off.

She was left staring out at the darkness beyond the windows and feeling a desolate sense of loss within.

Chapter Seven

She returned home, however, to the discovery of familiar things with unforeseen joy, as if her old self greeted her when she unlocked the door; here an ornament given to her in childhood, there a well-loved shelf of books. She had forgotten the cosiness of her carpeted lounge and the enfolding comfort of her armchairs. Outside, in the long, narrow strip of garden beyond the yard, she delighted in seeing yellow crocuses in the lawn, her lawn, and thick buds on her lilac tree.

In the kitchen there was a basket of fruit from the neighbours who had kept an eye on the house, and flowers and cards from colleagues at work. The phone rang incessantly as friends further afield welcomed her home. She soon realised how closed her life had been in Saint-André-sur-Audan, how bound up with only a few people, how dependent she had become upon them. Back in England she was free and at ease. She used the English idiom and was conscious of doing so, she heard familiar voices of radio broadcasters, saw familiar faces on television, drove her car, ate fish and chips and liquorice allsorts. In short, she resumed her life with new-found pleasure. Even her classes at school looked pleased to see her again.

She arranged penfriends for the French pupils, choosing for André a boy called Peter, the son of a butcher whose cheerful, outgoing family she knew well. She posted the first batch of letters off to Chantal who quickly sent her back a large envelope of replies in which there were also notes to her, including one from André to assure her he was still coming to England in July and to ask what he needed to bring.

It was not until mid-June though that she had a letter from Sylvie, signed also by Philippe, which said that André would indeed be travelling with Mademoiselle Boileau in July to stay with her and Peter's family, who had invited him. She said she agreed reluctantly to this trip but had been persuaded that her son would come to no harm.

A day or so before the scheduled arrival, the English woman received details from Chantal who would be travelling to Carlisle via Newcastle so as to be with André as far as Huntingdon where he could be collected.

And so it was that, having temporarily set aside the writing of reports, the young woman drove out across the fens late one sultry July afternoon to meet a child she had invited in a moment of rashness when, for no reason she could remember, he had meant something to her.

The figure that got off the train was smaller than she had recalled and looked vulnerable, even pathetic. She ran to him and kissed him, taking his case but finding it snatched from her hand again. Chantal, by the door, shouted, "I'll be in touch about the return journey," smiling and waving at them both as the train left. They followed the other passengers up over the footbridge and out by the ticket office, André giving monosyllabic answers to her questions. When they reached the car and put the case in the boot, he automatically walked round to the driver's side.

"Do you want to drive?" she asked, teasing. He smiled then, for the first time, as he ran to the other side.

During the journey, he looked with disbelief at the flatness of the landscape where sky and fields merged in a distant murky haze.

"We are actually below sea-level," she explained, "All this used to be under water and has been drained."

He nodded wearily. Now was not the time for a geography lesson. She began to ask about his family and he immediately livened up.

"My mother, my father, my aunt, my uncle and my three cousins all went to Pradoux station with me last night. There were two cars."

"Goodness, what a lot of people! It was late for the little girls."

"Nathalie, she cried because she did not like the train. My mother, she cried also."

"And you?"

"Oh no. I was very sad but I was also happy. Do you understand?"

"Yes, I understand."

On arrival at the house she phoned André's parents to let them know of his safe arrival. He spoke to them briefly in flat tones, audible but incomprehensible, before entering the kitchen where the table was already laid for a meal. He looked lost and lonely, with dark rings under his blue eyes giving all the signs of lack of sleep and dazed travelling. She put an arm round his shoulders and kissed his black hair, speaking to him in French.

"We're going to have a good time this week, just wait and see. And you and Peter will get on just fine. He and his family are planning to take you out to do all sorts of exciting things, when you're not in school, that is."

She continued her cheerful monologue throughout the meal. Afterwards, they exchanged presents. For her there was a scarf with scenes of the Audan valley and a book of the Central Massif which had a photograph of the village taken from the bridge. For him there was a miniature London bus, a book of puzzles and some sweets.

The next morning he was still quiet and after she had handed him over to Peter for the day she saw the English boy trying hard to make André smile, or if not smile, look less terrified. She saw them again at lunch-time queuing for their self-service meal, with André looking bemused amid a group of jolly girls vying for his attention as they practised their French on him. They did make him smile, but he still bore an air of staring fear.

That evening, Sylvie phoned. André's voice was lively this time and could be heard recounting his day. When at last he came into the kitchen he was relaxed, smiling, such as she had known him in France. More than ever she wanted to hug him, but from the other side of the table merely enquired about his parents.

"They are well. My father says he is very proud of me because I manage without my family and when I shall go home, no, when I go home," he grinned as he corrected himself, "we shall have a special meal at the hotel. Then I shall work for my uncle in the hotel, and my mother also."

"I am proud of you too, André," said the young woman, the bond between them almost tangible now.

The week went quite well. She showed him round the little town, took him to visit Peter's family, taught him how to wield a tennis racquet, let him have a go on all the stalls of a local church fête. On a trip to Peterborough they rode on a steam train and went shopping for souvenirs and presents. One day, he went to London with a group from school and came back weary but glowing having seen the sights known to him from posters and school-books.

He was due to go and stay with Peter's family for the second week, starting on the Friday. The previous evening, he was so unusually quiet, curled up in one of her armchairs, that she asked if everything was all right.

He said it was, then she saw the tears in his eyes. As one spilled gently over on to his cheek he wiped it away quickly with his sleeve.

"André, what is it?"

He shrugged.

"Tell me André. What's the matter?"

She moved over to him and knelt beside the chair, reaching out a hand to him. He flung his arms about her neck, sobbing on to her shoulder. She was not the teacher now; she could hold him, smooth his hair, rock him.

"I don't want to go to Peter's. Don't make me go."

"Oh André, why ever not?"

"I want to stay here with you."

The boy clung to her, fragile in her arms.

"But Peter's looking forward to having you. They all are. Don't you like them?"

"Yes, yes. But I want to stay here."

"There's nothing for you to do here. I know that you'll be going with the family to the seaside and they're also going to take you roller-skating and swimming and to the cinema. You'll have a really good time, you know, and you'll still see me at school, won't you?"

"It's not the same."

She insisted, however, pointing out that his own parents were expecting him to stay at Peter's.

"Look, I'll tell you what, go tomorrow as planned and stay the weekend with them. We can't spoil their plans now. Then on Tuesday you can come back here for the last two nights if you want. You'll have to sleep down here, though, because Mademoiselle Boileau is coming and needs the spare room. Okay?"

The boy lifted his head and nodded. Kissing her on both cheeks, he said,

"Thank you, Helen."

It was the first time he had called her by her name. Although it was natural that he should, the intimacy of the evening made her glad he was going to a family, with other children, instead of relying solely upon her.

So he left her on the Friday, but was back on the Tuesday, satisfied with his stay but relieved to be with her once more.

Together they drove to Peterborough to meet Chantal travelling from the north. Her arrival heralded the end of his stay; he was relaxed now, talking of the journey home, of his parents, of his relatives. In school the following day he was near-exuberant, proud to identify with his own French teacher who had come to visit her former pupils, staying by her during the sports afternoon and even going with her when she visited her former landlady in the evening. It was as if he no longer wanted the English woman's attention and she, having become used to guarding against his dependence upon her and backing off, was now the one reaching forward while he was in retreat.

When she got up very early on his final morning, he was already dressed and packed, with the bedding from his overnight sleep on the settee neatly folded by one of the arms. He watched her every movement as she prepared breakfast.

"Helen, when will you come back to France?"

"You mean to Saint-André-sur-Audan?"

"Of course."

"Well, you see I sometimes have a few days in Paris, but I hope I shall one day go back and see all my friends in Saint-André."

"You can stay in the hotel – or with us."

"Thank you, André. I'd really like to, you know that."

"If you come in summertime you will see a big difference. There are lots of persons – people – in the valley then. My father hates that, but my uncle in the hotel is very pleased. Are you coming in August?"

"Not this year, I'm afraid. I'd like to, but..."

She began to recognise a sense of loss within her, consuming all other emotion. The finality of the separation punched her below the ribs, taking away her appetite. She managed to sip a cup of tea while Chantal chatted happily, then she was in control of all the activity of loading the car, checking to see that nothing had been left behind and driving off to Huntingdon for an early train.

They waited on the breezy platform with people going about their daily routine while she stood with a hand on André's shoulder looking down the empty track and counting the remaining minutes. There was nothing about the train when it arrived to indicate its special importance. She embraced Chantal before kissing André and crushing him in her arms. Then she was left on the empty platform waving to a carriage of expressionless commuters hiding within their suited ranks a beloved child returning to his parents.

Chapter Eight

In retrospect the years pass quickly. Uncertainty and impatience prolong the unrelenting day-by-day unfolding of the continuous present stretching to a distant and unknown future, but the past is never so far away: last year, two years ago – it matters little; ten, twenty years ago is enough to give a rough frame in which to set a memory; the further back in time one looks, the closer the stages of the past become, like sleepers on a railway-track. Vagueness becomes an adequate definition: in the seventeenth or eighteenth century, in the Middle Ages, the Dark Ages, BC.

It is not the clock or the calendar which marks the passage of time, but the value put on events. Thus the mere arrival of a letter can take on the proportions of a major international event, depending on the personal impact. Nor is it marked so much by adults, but by the children – babies, toddlers, at school so soon – as if the older ones, watching, had stepped off the time-rails to see them grow.

The English woman had little to show in real terms for the eight years of contentment and frustrations since her stay in Saint-André-sur-Audan, except for her journeys to other countries for personal holidays and with school-trips to Paris.

Hopes of a visit to Saint-André were never realised and correspondence between the two schools waned, though Chantal had been to England several times, at first on her own and later, as Madame Cordesse, with her husband.

Each January she received new year's greetings from the Rodez and Massaud families, with a brief update of family news. Three years after her visit she was notified of the birth of Christophe, a brother for the three girls. It was hard to imagine how the children had grown. For her they stayed as photo images. As for Christophe, now already older than Laurence had been, she could only imagine a younger version of André. André himself had long since left school, having gone to the *lycée* in Pradoux where he had passed his *baccalauréat* before working with his father in winter and his uncle in summer. There had been no mention of the closure of the College, nor indeed of the furthering of Albert's plans. She could only assume that in Saint-André-sur-Audan life continued much as before.

Then one Friday, on returning home for a blessed weekend's sanctuary from school, she found a letter from André, in English. He hoped she was well and would have a good year; everything was going well for him and his family; he was really writing to ask if she knew of any hotel in England where he could work for a few months, until the end of May, as he needed more experience and wanted to practise his English; plans for the huge hotel complex had just been approved and work on the foundations would soon start; he was hoping to work there when it opened; he remembered very well the happy time he had spent in England eight years before; he would like to meet her again but perhaps she would not recognise him, as he was now twenty-one.

She hastily looked at herself in the mirror. Would he recognise her? Had she changed so much?

Clutching his letter she went out of the house again and drove off excitedly to the market place, where she parked by the lights of the old coaching inn on the corner. As soon as she approached Reception she was greeted by a former pupil at the desk.

"Hello, Miss Camberley. What can I do for you?"

"Is Mr Harding available?" She taught the proprietor's children and knew she would get a sympathetic hearing.

At his name he came and stood at the doorway by the reception desk. She put the letter on the counter and explained the circumstances.

"He would do anything, I know," she said. "He'd work in the kitchens, wash up, wait at table, serve in the bar, help with paper-work, even decorate a bedroom, anything." She remembered Albert's approach to hotel work and knew André would be well-trained and used to long hours.

"He sounds too good to be true," commented Mr Harding. "But as it happens, this winter we're going to be kept quite busy one way and another. We've got a film-crew booked in while they make a film on location in the high street. Look, I'll put him on a fortnight's trial, living in with basic pay, and let him do a bit of everything. No favours, mind. He could start next week if he wants, say Friday night.

He would have a day off a week and some time each day between two and five or six."

"That's great, Mr Harding. Thanks."

"Oh and tell him to speak French to that son of mine. I want him to do well at A-level."

"So do I," said the woman in mock indignation.

That evening she searched for André's phone number and having found it tapped it out with no little agitation.

"Allo?"

"Hello, Sylvie? It's Helen Camberley from England. Is André there, please?"

"One moment."

Then she was talking to him again, the boy of long ago who had made breakfast for her and had cried on her shoulder. Only it was a man's voice which greeted her.

"André? It's Helen. I've found a job for you, in a hotel near me. Can you start next Friday?"

"In a week? Oh, that's very soon. Just a minute."

She heard voices speaking quickly, then he said, "Yes, why not? Where is it exactly? Oh, that's very nice. I shall see you again."

"I can fetch you from the station provided it's after school. Give me a ring when you arrive in England."

She gave him her own and the school's numbers.

Within the week she was driving out across the fens, though this time in blustery darkness, to meet André at Huntingdon station. She stood by the footbridge, watching the train pull in and trying to pick him out among the alighting passengers. Was that him with the rucksack or the one with the suitcases?

She peered along the platform as a figure stood before her.

"Helen?"

There he was, tall and broad-shouldered.

"André!" she laughed in disbelief.

"I have changed, yes? You haven't."

"Wait till you see me in the light! Well, aren't you going to say hello?"

He kissed her without embarrassment.

"I am pleased to see you again."

"And I you, André. Come on. Is this your luggage?"

She took the handle of one of his holdalls and it linked them as they crossed over the bridge and went outside.

"Oh, it has all changed. Where's your car? I have a car now, you know. At least it's my mother's but I use it mostly. It's a Fiat."

They drove out of town and eventually emerged on the open fen, where the wind buffeted the car and the headlights picked out the long plumed rushes tossing and swaying in the dykes along the road-side.

"Is there snow at Mas Saint-André?"

"No, not this year."

"Has your father killed the pig yet?"

"We don't have one anymore."

"I remember eating black pudding at your home one Sunday."

"I remember you came to our house with my uncle and aunt and cousins."

"How is everyone?"

"Fine. They send their love and ask when are you going to visit them."

"That's nice. I'd like to see them all again. Your cousins will have changed a lot."

"Yes. Anne Sophie and Laurence are at the College now. They also like English. Nathalie is at primary school and Christophe is at nursery school."

"The College is still open, then."

"Yes, and M. Noiret is still the principal. There are more pupils now, nearly sixty."

"We have thirteen hundred."

"That's a lot."

She drove through the centre of the town to show him the hotel where he would start work the following evening. That night, though, he would spend in her spare room.

He expressed surprise that her house was smaller than he remembered, though otherwise his memory served him well. He went straight to the kitchen and filled the kettle. Switching it on, he said, "I am ready for a cup of tea."

He grinned boyishly and the woman briefly recognised the André of old, with his intense blue eyes and his black hair still swept back. She was suddenly aware of his youthful vulnerability.

"You'd better phone home," she said.

He pulled a face but did as she suggested while she checked the casserole and potatoes baking in the oven.

After the meal they sat in front of the gas fire and André talked, about the journey, about his family, about his work. All she had to do was to listen and watch, fascinated, tracing on the features of this young man the face of the boy she had once known. The quality of his English impressed her and she told him so.

"We have more and more people from Britain in the hotel," he explained. "I talk with them and they like that. Some speak French, of course, but not all. It is even possible to buy English newspapers in the village in summer and sometimes I read them."

"So the village is not dying?"

"Oh no, my uncle's plans are very good, I think."

"And your father?"

"My poor father, he is not pleased with what is happening but he has no choice. Did you know we have a vineyard now? He bought some land and has restored a terrace which I help him with. I prefer the hotel-work though, and so does my mother, but it is closed in winter."

"That's why you're here?"

"Yes, partly. Now you'd better tell me about this job you've found for me."

She explained the arrangements, which met with approval. He seemed confident, self-assured, at ease, and in vain she looked for the distraught child who had curled up in the same armchair and had sought comfort from her. He would not even remember it now, but nostalgia for that moment, for that child, crept deep within her and nestled there.

The next day he moved out to the hotel. It was with some surprise on the Saturday afternoon, then, answering a knock at the door, that she found André on the doorstep.

"What's the problem?" she asked, standing aside to let him in.

"Nothing. Everything is fine." He flung his jacket over the back of the chair and sat down, sprawling his legs out towards the fire. "I have some free time, so I thought I'd come and talk to you."

She was amused, but pleased, to have him there with her. It was a pattern so often repeated over the weeks that at times she had to apologise for not giving him her full attention; she had other things to do. He made himself completely at home, switching on the television or playing cassettes. He even helped at times with the hoovering or cleaning the windows. In the end she gave him a house key so that he could come and go as he pleased.

Mr Harding was full of praise for him and wished he could employ him permanently.

"He's a good lad, is André. Everybody likes him," he said. "I believe he brings in trade as well. He's popular with the young ones, especially the young ladies, when he's serving at the bar of an evening. He's learned very fast. And isn't his English good? Our Simon talks to him in French, of course, which is all good practice for him. Yes, it's working out well. I'm satisfied. Maybe one day there'll be an opportunity for Simon to go over to France for a while. It's a good idea, this work experience."

It was not so much about his work that André talked but about his home; he told her how he loved going hunting in the Cévennes mountains and how his father had once killed a wild boar; he spoke of Philippe's knowledge of the area, where to find the best cep mushrooms and the best sweet-chestnuts, where there were *avens* on the Causse, those holes in the limestone leading to underground grottoes with stalagmites and stalactites. He loved being with his father, following the old footpaths along the valley or ancient tracks across the plateaux. He had learned some Occitan – "not very much" – and had learned a lot about loving a land that was his. André spoke with pride about the hamlet of Mas Saint-André and the village by the Audan run by his uncle who, after being voted out of office for a while during the previous eight years, was now mayor again.

"André," she said one day when he had called round, "do you ever wish you had gone to university?"

"What for?"

"Why, to study English, or anything for that matter, just to get away and study with young people your own age."

"My parents did not want it."

"But you, André, did you?"

He thought for a moment. "Maybe when my friends from the *lycée* at Pradoux went to Montpellier I wanted to go with them, but what's the use? Being in a city, studying books, listening to lectures and writing essays, what would it teach me? Where would it lead me? I see my friends now and I do not envy them. They seem so young and they attach so much importance to their studies they look down on me, I'm sure they do."

"But wouldn't you like to be away from home?"

He grinned and again she glimpsed the boy in him.

"I'm here. Isn't that far enough away?"

Then he began to talk, as though she had unlocked a secret compartment and the contents came spilling out.

"To tell you the truth, Helen, I had to get away. I said it was for experience and that's true in part, but it's the winter that's the most difficult for me. I'm just stuck at home with my mother and father and the cat – do you remember Minet? In summer at the hotel there is always so much to do and so many people around that I am always busy. I work much harder than here. But in the long winter months I work sometimes with my father but I am living at home." He paused. "I have a problem with my mother. She wants to do everything for me. She makes my bed and tidies my room and chooses my clothes. I can't seem to do anything for myself. Then if I tell her off, she's upset. She monopolises me. She worries when I'm not there. Do you remember when I came to England before?"

"Of course!"

"She made me feel so guilty when I got back. I didn't understand at the time, naturally, but I do now. She told me she'd been ill with worry while I'd been away and it was the last time she'd consent to such a stupid idea. She was never interested in my holiday, you know. I couldn't talk to her about it. My father wanted to hear all about it, and so did my uncle and aunt, but not my mother. She blamed my aunt and my father and said it was their fault that I went to England."

"Did she blame me?"

"She never said so. She didn't talk about you. I don't think she's very happy about my being here now, but that's too bad. It's my life. She doesn't own me. I love her, of course, but I'm not a child any more. I feel I need to break free; is that how you say it?"

She nodded.

"I had a long letter from her today. She says I am forgetting my responsibilities to my family."

"What responsibilities?"

"According to her I am not writing or phoning often enough and she thinks that's because I don't care. But, Helen, I phone every week, and I write."

66

"That seems often enough to me."

"But you see she needs to be part of my life, involved in every part of it. Do you know she sent me a food parcel yesterday and here I am living in a hotel!"

"Perhaps she thinks English food is bad for you."

"Even so, it's for me to decide. Anyway, she also said I was not setting a good example to my cousins and I should be there with them."

"But they're at school."

"Exactly. One day they will travel and my aunt and uncle won't mind. Auntie Monique is lovely. She's so understanding. I think my mother envies her."

"Surely not. Your mother is also very nice and, from what I remember, very beautiful."

"Yes, she is, but Auntie Monique has daughters and my mother couldn't have children after me. She didn't mind too much because she enjoyed being an aunt to the girls, but now there's Christophe, she's really jealous."

"That's a strong word, André."

"Well, it's true. She was proud to have a son. Then Auntie Monique had daughters *and* a son of her own."

"And a hotel."

"And a hotel," he repeated. "I think it is worse as well because my uncle Albert is so important in the village and has good ideas, whereas my father is rather old-fashioned in his views. My mother does not like that. It makes her angry sometimes, and then my father is sad and goes out. Then she is more angry and says he doesn't face up to things. Life can be hard at home sometimes."

"Perhaps your mother is going through a difficult time, André. Some women her age do, you know. Try not to judge her too harshly."

"You don't know my mother. She needs to be in control and to own people, so that they do what she wants."

"Maybe she's insecure."

"Maybe. That doesn't help me. Oh, you won't tell her what I've said, will you?"

"Don't be silly."

"Or my father or aunt or uncle?"

"As if I would. What chance have I got?"

"If you come to Saint-André-sur-Audan in summer."

"I'd not considered it."

"Well, why not? You could go to the hotel as before."

"Maybe. I'll think about it."

After that he spoke freely to her about his family, discussing with her the contents of letters or telephone conversations. Of his life at the local hotel, however, he said little. She knew he had found friends with whom he sometimes spent his days off. He gave no further details and she asked no questions, not wanting to make his mother's mistakes. He had settled happily into his work, adapting fully to the English way of life.

Just before Easter he spent a day in Cambridge with Peter, his erstwhile penfriend, who had come down from Leeds University. The city, and in particular its colleges, obviously had an effect on André for when he next visited her he spoke of the old stones and tranquil paved courtyards with a reverence normally kept for his own village. She took him there herself to wander where in the name of academic pursuit vaults of stone arched overhead and lawns stretched vast and trim to the little river gliding softly under the bridges. They went into bookshops in which thousands of books created an atmosphere all of its own, and people reacted accordingly, speaking in hushed tones.

Back home, she selected a novel from her bookcase.

"Here, read this and see what you think."

"I've not got much time."

"I know, but look at it anyway. I like it."

She handed him *The Go-Between*.

He turned it over in his hands. "I'm not a great reader," he said, "but I'll take it."

Within a week he had brought it back having read it and asked to borrow another. She chose again from her collection, luring him book by book.

One day he was quieter than usual. It was not out of tiredness, he said, but he had realised his time in England was running out. He was happy in the hotel, with the Harding family and with his friends. He wanted to stay.

"I don't want to go back, Helen, really I don't. I have my own life and my own job. I don't want to depend on my family. I like being here. I am free."

"I didn't want to come back to England when I was in France," she said, "but once I'd got back it was fine. Don't worry."

"Did you have nightmares? Me, I have nightmares. I dream that I am back in Mas Saint-André or in the Hotel de l'Audan and I wake up very sad until I see that I'm still in England. One night I dreamed there were crocodiles in the Audan and they came into the hotel. No, don't laugh. It was so real. It has put me off going home."

"Your family would be upset to hear that."

"I shan't tell them. Oh Helen, can't I stay? I'd do anything to stay here."

"No, André, no. You can come here as often as you like, you know that, but your place is over there. It's a beautiful region with a rich history and hopefully an exciting future. You've forgotten what it's like to be there."

"No, I haven't. It wouldn't be so bad if I could be treated as an adult. Here, I'm not treated as a child, but there, I'm still the 'little André' they've always known. I want to be treated like my uncle Albert, not like my cousins."

"Maybe things will be different when you go back. You may find their attitude has changed as well."

"No, no. My mother won't change." He leaned forward and put his head in his hands, running his fingers through his black hair as he did so. "Oh Helen, what should I do?"

"Look, there are a few weeks left yet. Don't worry. You'll feel different when you go back. Wait and see."

She stood up and ruffled his hair as she passed him to go to the kitchen.

"Cup of tea?"

"What do you say? It's the pana... panacea for all ills? Is that it?"

"It kills crocodiles."

"Ha!"

He came to her in the kitchen and kissed her on both cheeks for the first time since the greeting at the station.

"Oh, Helen, you're great."

She pushed him playfully. "Don't be daft."

One afternoon she slipped out of school during a free period to pay in a cheque. She was just approaching the bank when she spotted, on the opposite side of the road, a young couple holding hands as they walked along. They stopped outside an estate agent's where the young man took the girl in his arms and kissed her before she went in. The girl she recognised by the long blond hair as a former pupil called Stephanie who worked there. The man was André.

She quickly walked through the doors to the bank before André turned. She was confused, disturbed, let down. She knew André had friends; she had preferred by not asking questions not to think of them, but rather to deny in effect their existence. It was unrealistic of her not to admit he was close to others of a similar age to himself. Now his reluctance to return to France was understood. It was Stephanie, a beautiful girl sixteen years her junior, who had won his heart. He had not spoken of her. Whilst sharing his thoughts on his family, he had kept his private life in England to himself. She felt cheated, rejected and hurt.

The next time he called she watched him warily to see whether he showed any sign of his involvement with the girl. He was his normal self, though subdued as before, again saying he wanted to stay. He said he had heard from his uncle who was expecting him back soon.

"My mother even sent me money for the fare back. That annoys me, it really does."

"But will you go?"

"I suppose so."

"Good, because I've definitely made up my mind. I'll go to Saint-André-sur-Audan in August – if there's a room available in the hotel, that is."

"Oh yes, my uncle and aunt will find one for you, I'm sure."

"So we'll meet again in France. Does that please you?"

"You know I shall be working. We all shall."

"That doesn't matter, does it? I'll sit by the river all day."

"It's too hot."

"I won't go if you don't want me to."

"I do. It will be nice for you to see the village again. A lot of people remember you."

*

Just before his departure he visited her in different mood. He was humming and singing around the house and his face looked different, tired but smiling and less drawn than of late, more adult, more masculine. She thought of his relationship with Stephanie, obviously closer than the one with herself, who had the greater claim. She became indulgent, as if taking credit for allowing him to have the relationship with the girl. She was glad now that he was leaving but that she would soon see him again, surrounded by his family. Heaven forbid that he should want to stay in England for ever, for the sake of Stephanie with the long blond hair.

He left, contentedly. She had asked him if he wanted to invite anyone to share his farewell meal at her house. He had said not. Did he want anyone to go to the station with them? No. He had never spoken of Stephanie, but talked increasingly of what he would do back in France and of what presents he had bought for his family. He had given her his full attention on the last afternoon, sitting beside her on the settee, showing her some of the photos he had taken in England and kissing her affectionately before leaving for his last night at the hotel. The next morning she had taken him to Huntingdon station, dropping him off by the booking hall. He had kissed her goodbye, had taken his luggage out of the boot, then had kissed her again.

"See you in August!"

"See you in August!"

As she drove away she glanced in the rear-view mirror, but he had already disappeared into the station. She turned right at the traffic lights and headed through the town and back across the serene, blue-skied fens for another normal day's work. No one was to notice that she felt bereft.

Chapter Nine

After three weeks without any contact from France since André's departure the woman was left to assume that his life at home had absorbed him totally and she was forgotten. Driven by determination not to be utterly rejected, she wrote to Albert and Monique asking for accommodation for a week in August, provided someone could collect her from Pradoux station. The 'someone' she hoped would be André.

Within a fortnight she received an answer of such a warm and generous nature, since she would not be charged as a hotel guest but invited as one of the family, that she chided herself for her feelings about André's lack of correspondence. There was even a word from Sylvie at the bottom of Albert's letter, which thanked her for her help during her son's stay in England and which told her he was very busy working for his uncle.

It was comforting to know that Mr Harding had heard nothing from him either. She thanked him as if she was passing on gratitude from André's parents and he seemed satisfied with that.

"Even his girl – you know Stephanie, don't you? – even Stephanie hasn't heard from him. She kept asking me if I'd had a letter or a phone-call. She'd tried phoning, I think, but he was never there at the time. Anyway, it doesn't matter now. She comes in here with her new boyfriend. He was a nice lad, was André. A good worker. He knew what the job was about. If he got something out of his time here, that's the main thing. I'd like someone to do the same for my son Simon one day."

It seemed a long while until August. She was annoyed with herself for allowing the rhythm of her routine to be disturbed. She wasn't used to such intensity of anticipation which cast a shadow of insignificance over the days other than that they were drawing her nearer to her return to Saint-André-sur-Audan and to the young man with whom she had shared special moments recently and all those years ago. All her living went into the thought of her arrival, ever supported by memories of times past repeated in her mind with increasing importance.

The day of the departure came. She existed through the journey to the coast, across the Channel and on to Paris where she changed stations, as she had done over eight years before. Paris was hot, and the train stuffy. She slept fitfully, her excitement rising as the train sped south. She recalled with pleasure those same sensations as the train stopped at the same stations and rattled over the same long viaduct. When she alighted at the little station it was daylight and there stood a figure to meet her. It was not André.

"Albert!"

"Hello, Helen. Did you have a good journey?" He kissed her then stood back with his hands on her shoulders to look at her. "You've not changed a bit."

"Neither have you."

The train slid past them. Albert picked up her case and together they went through the little building with its same wooden floor and to the car.

"Do you remember the snow the last time you met me at the station?"

"Oh yes, I do now. You will find everything very different in summer. It gets stiflingly hot in the valley and there are lots of people."

"That's good. It means work for you all."

"Did André tell you the complex is going ahead? The foundations are in already. They're beginning on the walls. You'll see. Do you remember André's father, Philippe? He's a builder on the site."

"Really? Does that mean he's come to terms with tourism?"

"Needs must, Helen. But he's not a happy man."

She enquired about the rest of the family and learned that Monique, little Christophe and Nathalie had stayed to see her but were leaving later that day to go to stay with relatives by the sea near La Grande Motte. The older girls were working at the hotel.

As before, they drove up over the hills. As before, Albert swerved to the edge of the road so that his passenger looked straight down into the ravine far, far below. Despite herself, since she was prepared this time, she gave a start.

"It's even more impressive than I remembered," she said as they drove on. This was true also of their descent to the village. They drove past the bridge where André had sat with his stick, and past the row of riverside shops and cafés whose owners were winding up their metal blinds and setting displays and tables outside.

She was nervous as she entered the hotel where she was greeted first by Monique and the girls, with their bemused little brother, and then by Sylvie. Of André there was no sign. It was Anne Sophie and Laurence who proudly gave her breakfast and showed her to her room. As before, she slept, but this time there was an emptiness she had not experienced then.

She awoke to the realisation that she could not hear the river Audan flowing through the valley, but noises of car engines and shouting and voices of children. On opening the shutters, she saw why. Where in winter the Audan had flowed, cars were parked, bright ranks of them glinting garishly under the onslaught of the sun. The river had shrunk back to a band of green water creeping round the cliffs opposite, widening into shallow pools here and there where children splashed and squealed. On the walls by the bridge and along the parapet sat people. Tourists! She resented their intrusion instinctively.

Downstairs in the restaurant she encountered Sylvie who showed her to a table in the corner by the kitchen door and handed her a menu. The English woman took it, but instead of reading it, glanced about her as Sylvie moved away. The windows at the end were open on to a terrace with tables shaded by colourful parasols. She watched as Sylvie approached a group of men seated at one of the tables. Then a tall figure rose and walked into the restaurant towards her.

"Philippe!" She leaped to her feet.

"Hello, Helen. How are you?"

He kissed her in greeting and she was pleased, smiling at him as he stood back to look at her with those blue eyes.

"I'm fine. It's good to see you again. How are things with you?"

"Alas, Helen, I adapt badly to change. You've heard about the new hotel complex for the village?"

"Yes, it's up the valley, isn't it? I saw the site when I was here before. Aren't you working on it?"

"Ironic, isn't it? Here I am having to build for tourists."

"And for the village."

He shook his head. "In theory, that's true. But..." He paused. "Enough of that. I've not thanked you for all you did for my son. He seems to have enjoyed his stay in England. He's more settled now than he was before, more self-assured, more adult. It did him good to get away."

"No hard feelings about English, then?"

"Oh, don't hold that against me. No, no. Of course, if only you could speak Occitan..." He was teasing her and they laughed together.

"Have you chosen yet?" It was Sylvie for her order.

"I'll have melon and then ratatouille, please."

Philippe rejoined the group of men on the terrace. Shortly afterwards they shifted their chairs, got up and strolled across the road to a café where they regrouped.

The English woman, despite encouraging smiles from Anne Sophie and Laurence as they edged their way to and from the kitchen between the tables, was conscious of eating alone. She took a piece of bread from the basket in front of her, pulling small bits off in her fingers and taking them to her mouth until the half-melon filled with port arrived and she forgot her isolation in the sheer pleasure of its fresh taste and smooth texture. She scraped out the flesh of the melon until only the outer skin remained. Sylvie whipped it away and placed the ratatouille on the table. The woman was longing to ask about André. She had glanced around the restaurant several times. He was not there. Nor was he at the café opposite.

She finished the ratatouille, using her bread to soak up the last traces of juice.

"Cheese or dessert?"

"I'd like fruit tart. Of course."

This made Sylvie smile.

'When she returns with it,' thought the woman, 'I'll ask her about André.'

"One fruit tart."

"Thank you, Sylvie. By the way, is André okay? I've not seen him yet."

"It's his day off. He's out with friends."

"He knew I was coming today?"

"Of course. He'll be back at work tomorrow. You'll see him then."

So, he knew and had chosen not to be there. She felt let-down and humiliated in front of his mother who could see that this time her arrival in the village was of no consequence to him.

After the meal she went out into the village to join the thronging tourists. That was all she was, after all. An outsider, a tourist. What was it Philippe once said? "Tourists destroy what they come to find."

She walked on to the old bridge, stopping to sit on the parapet where she had last stood alone, feeling its strength. There was now an endless stream of cars zigzagging down the Causse and entering the village, either to cross the bridge or to park by the river. Some had music blaring from their open windows, with the thud, thud of the beat fading into the general hubbub of the crowds as it passed. Below the bridge, where the might of the Audan was confined to its narrow passage skulking by the cliffs, yellow canoes darted under the arch which echoed with the occupants' shouts and laughter. By the edge, children waded into the water, shrieking and scooping up the surface to send a fountain of shiny droplets into the air; others ventured into deeper pools to swim. It was hardly the same river she had known. Yes, it was destroyed, tamed.

The village too had lost its peaceful charm, with its crowds eddying and flowing along the row of shops. As she went by, the woman tried to peer inside in the hopes of spotting a familiar face behind the counter. In vain. People were pushing in and out of doorways. Outside the bureau de tabac where holiday-makers pressed round the postcard stands, the queue extended beyond the door and became confused with the customers for the waffles stall. There were shops she did not know existed: shops selling shorts and T-shirts and sunhats, shops selling trinkets made in China and "local specialities" made goodness knows where, shops which would lock their shutters at the end of the season for their wares to be taken away to be sold at winter sports resorts. She felt a surge of sympathy for Philippe's values and left the river front to seek the shade and calm of the steep, narrow streets leading to the College.

The smells from the pizzeria on the corner accompanied her up the first alley where she came across more gift-shops. She continued upwards, leaving the crowds who ventured no further than the last shop, until she chanced upon only the occasional tourist turning a camera on to the old buildings decked with red geraniums or on to a sudden view down the valley.

The gates of the College were firmly closed, keeping her out. Inside was a former life with eager-eyed pupils, and one in particular.

She turned, rejected, and made for a bench high above the village. A couple sitting there moved on as she approached so she was able to claim it and look down at Saint-André, its huddle of roofs hiding its shame of tourism, though by the river the glint of sunlight on metal contrasted sharply with the brown of the dry landscape. She scanned the terraces, searching vainly for the one worked by Philippe and his son.

The heat was too intense for her to stay long. She went down the alleys and steps, emerging at the post office and bought a drink at the stall opposite.

Why had she come? What was she going to do? The week stretched before her like a desert, arid and barren. But tomorrow, tomorrow, she would see André.

She trailed back to the hotel which was empty and quiet now and lay on her bed, hands behind her head, staring at the ceiling in the dim, shuttered light. She ought not to have come, not alone, that is. But she had not wanted to share the village with anyone from England as they would not have understood her depth of feeling for it. The village though had moved on since her stay, without her. It was not as it had been. She should have realised.

She dozed for awhile in fitful reverie until her senses were alerted to the opening of a door on to the corridor and to voices she recognised, those of Albert and Monique, no Sylvie, as they went towards the stairs.

How could she be a mere tourist when André's family made her welcome? She recalled how they had greeted her, Philippe especially, and she smiled to herself. She was tired after the journey, that was what it was, making her oversensitive to André's absence.

She got up and left the hotel again, joining tourists who were not, like her, invited guests of the mayor.

The next morning she awoke early in excited anticipation and entered the restaurant before most of the other guests. She spotted him immediately, of course: André, smart and handsome in the black and white waiter's uniform. She sat and fixed her gaze on him until he turned and saw her. He came straight across to her, kissing her on both cheeks, singling her out from other guests. She beamed in pride and pleasure.

"Did you enjoy yourself yesterday?"

"Yes. I went out with friends. And you, did you have a good journey?"

"Yes thanks. I am happy to be here again."

"Coffee? Or tea perhaps?"

"Coffee." She was taken aback by the abrupt end to any hope of conversation.

He returned with a coffee pot, a jug of hot milk, a length of bread, butter, jam and a croissant.

"Remember the first time you served me my breakfast in Saint-André?" André looked vague but answered "Yes" before moving on to a German family who had come to sit at the next table. She heard him asking them if they had enjoyed their canoeing trip down the river the previous day and watched him as he responded to their enthusiasm.

She did not have chance to speak to him again, nor did he so much as glance in her direction.

At lunch-time she was served by Sylvie. Once André looked at her as he came out of the kitchen and asked if she was okay.

"I'm okay." What else could she say? Could she stand up in a roomful of people and shout, as she wanted to, that of course she was not okay and why was he treating her like a stranger, an outsider, after all she'd done, after all those intimate conversations? Why couldn't he show that she meant something to him, that they had a special relationship which went beyond waiter and guest? At every opportunity Sylvie placed a free hand on his shoulder as they passed, as she did to her brother-in-law Albert, but acted as a barrier between them and the English woman.

Slowly the days passed. One morning Albert had to go to Pradoux and took his daughters and the woman with him for the journey. She bought a couple of second-hand paperbacks from a stall on the market and spent the next day or so in the shade of the willow tree by the river, reading them.

One evening, when fewer people were around, she popped into the butcher's and introduced herself. The butcher's wife came rushing round from behind the counter to greet her, delight obvious on her face, and called her husband. They complained of their long hours of work in summer and of the number of tourists but it was good for business. Even in winter trade was better than it used to be as visitors came to the valley all year round now.

"It's progress," said the butcher with a resigned shrug of the shoulders. "Tourism is our livelihood. Between you and me," he went on with a glance at his wife, "tourists are less choosy than villagers. We can call anything a local speciality and they'll buy it."

"Do they buy your *fricandeau*?" asked the English woman.

"They buy what we call *fricandeau*. The real *fricandeau* we keep for the locals. Why waste good stuff on tourists?"

They all laughed in a shared contempt which made the English woman realise that they at least did not count her among the hundreds of outsiders invading Saint-André-sur-Audan each day.

This gave her the courage to confront André after dinner much later that night after she, Anne Sophie, Laurence, Albert, Sylvie and André had been relaxing round a table on the terrace. Usually the English woman had left the group first, feeling excluded as the others discussed that day's work and the day ahead. This time she stayed. The girls went to their room first, leaving the others sipping the last of the wine and looking across at the floodlit bridge and cliffs.

"Not meeting your friends tonight, my darling?" Sylvie asked her son.

"Not tonight."

"Well, I'm suffocating here. There's no air. I'm going for a walk. Are you coming Albert?"

Suddenly they were gone, leaving the English woman alone with André. She turned on him at once.

"What's up with you? You've been treating me like a stranger."

"No, I haven't. I've been working."

"You've been avoiding me. Don't deny it."

He slumped across the table, pushing his fingers through his hair.

"Oh Helen, it's not easy. It's not you. Well, not exactly."

She waited. Eventually he went on, "I've got to come to a decision. No one knows yet. I can't spend another winter at home. I'm thinking of enrolling in October to study English at the Faculty."

"In Montpellier?"

"Of course."

"That's great! But why avoid me?"

"You are part of the equation. You have always encouraged me. You are an influence."

"You flatter me now. But you ignore me in front of your mother. That has nothing to do with English. Do you really like me?" She stressed the word 'really'.

"Of course. You know I do."

"Show me."

He looked at her.

"I am very fond of you, André. I thought we had a good understanding but you've been treating me like a stranger. If you like me, show me."

There, she had flung down a challenge for him to respond or humiliate her. He hesitated, then scraped his chair back and came to her side, stooping to kiss her on both cheeks, twice. She lifted her hands and slid her fingers through his hair before he drew away. He sat beside her, covering her hand with his. Tears welled up in her eyes and she brushed them away with her free hand.

"I've always been fond of you, Helen. You know that."

"As fond of me as of Stephanie?"

The mention of her name appeared to startle him and he withdrew his hand.

"So you knew? That was different. It's not the same thing at all."

"Why not?"

"Stephanie was..."

"Young?"

"Yes... no... I mean, more my age. I respect you very much, but it's not the same. You are like... a member of the family, a favourite aunt perhaps."

It was the best thing and the worst thing he could have said. They were playing this game again, of reaching out and of withdrawing, of somehow never meeting at a point which satisfied them both at the same time.

"Then please acknowledge me as one," she said simply.

"Okay. But don't tell anyone about the university idea."

"As if I would."

At least now she had his secret to cherish. She knew something of which Sylvie was unaware. The thought comforted her.

They sat in silence for a while. Albert and Sylvie did not return from their walk and the woman commented on the fact.

"Maybe they have stopped at a café in the village. Sometimes my father comes down from Mas Saint-André. Then he likes to go home to sleep. My mother usually stays here when she's working. It's more convenient. She has a little room in the annexe."

The explanation struck the English woman as odd but she made no comment. She recalled the voices on her first afternoon. They had come out of the same room on her corridor. Sylvie was spending more time with Albert than with Philippe. And Monique was away. It all began to make sense: Sylvie saw Albert as the successful hotelier and mayor; Philippe was a loser, unable to keep up with the present, but a deep thinker for all that. Moreover Sylvie was jealous of her sister, Monique. André had said as much during his stay in England. The thing was, did André realise what was going on, if anything was going on?

She recalled how years before Sylvie had paid more attention to Albert than to her own husband and, as André knew, how she needed to be in control of situations and of people around her.

"What are you thinking? Helen?"

"Nothing in particular. And you?"

"The same. I'm going to my room to read now."

They went upstairs together and parted on the first landing. The woman decided to wait up and listen for Albert's and Sylvie's return, but the heat of the evening, the wine and the reassurance of André's affections, albeit for a favourite aunt, conspired against her wishes and she slept soundly.

Chapter Ten

The following day, 15th August, was a Bank Holiday, drawing even more traffic to the village.

"It's the beginning of the end," said André, setting down the coffee pot at breakfast. "There'll be fewer people after today as they head for home. Besides, from 15th August the weather changes."

"Well, I hope it waits to change until after 17th," said the English woman. "I'm catching the night train."

"I know. It's my day off. I'm going to Montpellier with friends."

She was seized with a sudden empty panic. "Don't forget to say goodbye."

He seemed to understand what she meant. "I won't. Have a good day today."

What constituted a good day? He had no idea of the torture of waiting to see him and now the added torture of more time to kill before they could talk again, and then only to say goodbye, maybe for ever. But if he did go to university to study English, the link could possibly be maintained.

What was it about him that tormented her so, that had always tormented her? She watched him deftly move around the tables, holding aloft the breakfast trays; she longed to touch him, to claim him as hers, not Sylvie's. This time he would not implore her to take him back to England with her. And even if he did return with her, what of Stephanie, new boyfriend or not?

As André had said, it was the beginning of the end.

She had not seen Philippe to speak to since her first day. She was thinking of him and of his possible reaction to André's departure from his roots as she left the hotel after breakfast and found herself heading away from the bustle of the holiday crowds along the road to the building site where he would be working. Already the heat was intense, the sun relentlessly striking the rock-face out of which the road was carved. Once she had gone beyond the village boundary no tree offered her shade and there was no pavement. Cars whizzed by in a flurry of dust. She edged her way along the road-side through the glaring, gritty heat until she reached the track leading down towards the Audan and she stood at the top of it.

The whole site was a concrete scar, right down to where the Audan flowed, bare and exposed. The area had been cleared of trees, not only for the foundations of the hotel complex, but for the vehicles, machinery, equipment and materials which had laid siege to the natural landscape. In a haze of dust, cement mixers churned, engines revved, men shouted. Breeze-block after breeze-block the walls were growing as she watched.

On the other side of the track a board announced the Saint-André-sur-Audan hotel and leisure centre complex, to be open by next summer, and showed a drawing of a massive building dominating the valley, with international flags flying.

Albert had boasted that his idea was bringing life to the valley. Death would have been a more appropriate word, she thought miserably, with a deepening sense of foreboding. She would not return. Nothing would ever be the same again. Philippe had been right all along in wanting to maintain tradition and he had been scorned. What irony indeed that he was working on the valley's destruction. Poor, poor man. And there would be worse to come, with André leaving. What of Sylvie, too, spending so much time with Albert?

Back in the village she went and sat at the back of the medieval church. Outside she had experienced the searing heat, the glare of light, the dizzy thronging of the crowds. Inside it was cool and dark.

"Well, well, if I'm not mistaken it's the young lady from England, isn't it?"

She turned and recognised the old priest. She could have hugged him. They shook hands warmly and exchanged pleasantries.

"You are not too bored now," he said. "Saint-André-sur-Audan is full of life in summer."

"I was never bored," she protested with a smile. "I prefer the village as it was, in winter. There are too many people now, strangers who come here and spend their time in the shops. They are not interested in the village itself."

"Ah, mademoiselle, or should I say madame? No? Mademoiselle, you speak like one of us, of the older generation. Philippe Massaud, you know him of course, he understands. But no one can stop progress. More people means more money for trade, so the village survives."

"I know, but all the same..."

They stood a while in companionable silence before she made her excuses and left, returning to the river-front via cobbled tunnels where wet sheets were hung along a wire fixed to the wall.

She took a long siesta in her room, hearing the joyful cries of the children in the Audan but listening for any noise in the corridor. Somewhere a door clicked but on looking out she saw no one. Another time she glanced out and saw Anne Sophie and Laurence, in shorts, leaving their room.

"We're going swimming. Do you want to join us?"

"Thanks but no thanks. Have fun."

After that she left her door very slightly ajar. Eventually a door clicked open. Albert came out, followed by Sylvie who pulled the door to.

It took further evidence to convince the English woman that her suspicions were founded. That night she, Albert, Sylvie and the girls sat round the table on the terrace. André, it appeared, was having a late dinner with his father and staying in Mas Saint-André, where it was less stifling than in the valley. Sylvie had not accompanied him, on the pretext of preparing the next day's desserts. She and Albert got up to go to the kitchen. The girls were shooed away to bed and the English woman followed, but not before she had turned and glimpsed the two adults close together in an intimate embrace.

About midnight a light came on in the corridor. Albert and Sylvie arrived, unlocked the door and went inside. When the corridor light went out automatically, a trace of light could be seen under the door for a while, then it too was extinguished.

So there it was. Albert and Sylvie were having an affair. Not for the first time the English woman wished she had not come to Saint-André-sur-Audan for a holiday. She was suffering a whole gamut of emotions. She wanted to be at home again, leading her own life, not spying on other people's, not knowing secrets such as Sylvie's affair and André's decision, both of which would have such a devastating effect on the family. She wanted nothing more to do with them, with the village. She was weary of them all. And yet... she still felt her relationship with André was incomplete, unresolved. She had power over him now, sharing his secret and knowing what he did not know

about his mother. She felt a mixture of anguish and delight –
schadenfreude – which excited her.

The next day was to be her last with André. He was attentive to
her, serving her breakfast and she had the time to enquire after his
health.

"He's okay, all things considered."

She knew however it wasn't "all things". Philippe would have
other considerations to take into account.

The weather was hotter than ever and the village suffocatingly
airless. Anne Sophie and Laurence had been given the day off and this
time the English woman accepted their invitation to swim and have a
picnic lunch. They carried their baskets over the bridge, along a track
at the foot of the cliffs which led to the entrance to a camp-site and
beyond it to a fence marked *Private*.

"It's all right," said Laurence. "It's ours."

They followed a path through the leafy shade of the trees and came
out into a clearing where the Audan spread itself in lazy pools beyond
its main current. From time to time, parties of cheery canoeists sped
by, carried more by the flow of the river than by their attempts to
paddle. High above, on the other side, the road zigzagged down from
the top of the Causse before it disappeared round an outcrop of rocks
to approach the village from behind.

"This is Dad's next project," said Anne Sophie.

"What is?"

"This place. It will be ideal for a sports centre, don't you think?"

The English woman picked up a flat pebble and skimmed it across
the water. It made contact four times before it sank. The ripples
spread out and overlapped.

"I like it as it is."

Laurence laughed. "You sound like Uncle Philippe. He's always
saying that. We'll still be able to swim here. There'll be more
facilities, that's all."

They paddled at the water's edge with shrieks of mock surprise at
the chill of the water on their hot feet. The girls then fell flat into the
pool, sending up arcs of water which shattered and fell in a tingling
spray on their guest. She waded in, feeling the stones beneath her feet,
then ducked suddenly until her shoulders were under the surface of the
water. She turned on her back and floated, squinting upwards to the
blue intensity of the sky above the cliffs.

What would happen if the girls ever found out? Did their mother suspect? Was that why she had absented herself? Albert had such plans for the future and Sylvie backed them. She always had. They would control their own future and by doing so control that of others. Well, it happened, it happened all the time. It wasn't for her to get herself involved. She turned on to her front and swam towards the edge again. If only she didn't know what she knew, if only she didn't feel this longing mixed with dread at seeing André for the last time – heaven forbid that he would forget – this would be the happiest time of her holiday.

During the picnic the girls filled her in on details about the College, how Madame Cordesse, Chantal, had moved to St Flour and now had twin sons, how Monsieur Noiret, who was a "really old man" would soon be retiring, how her former flat was now the school library with books "even in English". In a year, Anne Sophie would be starting at the *lycée* in Pradoux, as a weekly boarder. She was looking forward to that.

"And then... university?"

Anne Sophie pulled a face. "Maybe a management course, to help my parents in the hotel business."

"Good idea." What else could she say?

They eventually wandered back past the camp-site where they were invited to join a game of volleyball. The English woman declined and returned to the hotel to shower and prepare herself for the evening, for the last goodbye to André.

He was serving in the restaurant, but not at her table. It was his mother who took her order and served up the dishes. The English woman met his eye once or twice and he acknowledged her with a slight tip of the head. Surely, surely he would not avoid her. He could not humiliate her again. But when all the work was done after the restaurant closed, only Albert and Sylvie appeared on the terrace. The girls had already gone to their room and André, to the English woman's chagrin, had, according to his mother, gone drinking with friends.

So he could not even stay to be with her, to say a final goodbye. She meant nothing to him, nothing, and judging by Sylvie's contented air as she passed on the information, his mother knew it too.

Her disappointment wove itself rapidly into a huge ball of anger, consuming all but her calm outward appearance. Anger at André for letting her down, anger at herself for allowing him to disturb her emotions, anger at Sylvie, so pretty and smug with her darling son and her lover, anger at Albert for deceiving Philippe and his own family. Wasn't he also deceiving everyone in the village with his use of power? He was destroying everything and everyone around him with his selfish plans and charming smile.

"This time tomorrow..." said Albert to her.

"... I'll be in the train," she finished. She wished it could be now. There was nothing left to stay for.

"Philippe will take you to the station. I can't leave the hotel at that time, what with André away."

"Don't worry. That's fine, thanks." She was glad it would be Philippe.

Sylvie stood up. "The air is so heavy. Let's go for a little stroll, Albert."

"Would you like a walk, Helen?" asked Albert. The woman stared at him in amazement. To what lengths would his deception go?

"No thanks. I'm going to my room. Goodnight."

Having prepared for bed she was about to switch off the lamp when there was a knock at the door.

"Helen? It's André."

She leapt up to open the door. He stood there, wearing only shorts and trainers.

"I've come to say goodbye, as I said I would."

"Oh, André!"

In one moment all was forgiven. He stepped inside and pushed the door to without closing it. She kissed him on the cheek and smelled the alcohol on his breath as he returned the embrace.

"So, you leave tomorrow. Have a good journey home."

"You too, to Montpellier. And good luck with your studies."

"And with telling my parents."

"That as well."

"Give my love to England."

"And to Stephanie?"

"Not especially."

"She has another boyfriend now."

"That's good."

"Is this the last goodbye? We may never see each other again."

"Don't say that."

"But it's true."

"You can come back here, to my uncle's hotel."

"Never." The word came out immediately, emphatically, too emphatically.

"You've not been happy here, Helen? Is it me? I thought I explained."

"It's not that."

"It's my mother, isn't it? Has she upset you?"

"No, not exactly. Oh, André."

"What is it?"

"Tell me, what is the relationship between your mother and your uncle?"

"My mother is the sister of Monique, Albert's wife. You know that."

"And you know perfectly well what I mean. You're a man now, not a child."

"They work together, that's all."

"No, André, no. More than that. Much more."

"You are not saying my mother and my uncle are having... an affair? That's ridiculous. You are wicked to say such a thing."

"I am wicked to say it, perhaps, yes. But it is true."

There, she had told him, she had given him her parting gift, her Parthian shot. And now all she wanted to do was to go alone miserably to bed and wake up in England as if nothing had happened.

"I've seen them, André. They go together to your uncle's room."

"That's impossible. My mother sleeps in the annexe."

"No, André. She now sleeps over there, across the corridor, with your uncle."

She pulled the door ajar to point into the darkness of the corridor. At that moment the light went on. She stepped across the room to switch off her bedside lamp and let him watch as she had watched the previous night.

He stood still for so long that eventually she reached out into the darkness to feel if he was still there. His skin was cold and clammy.

"André?" she whispered as she closed the door.

She felt the heave of his shoulders as he began sobbing, silently, against the wall and was conscious of her own searing pain of what she had done to him. She spoke soothingly to him, almost inaudibly, as she would to a child who had grazed his knee.

"It's okay. It'll be all right. It's a shock, I know." Then with an arm tightly round him she coaxed him through the darkness to her bed where he sat for a moment then turned to clutch the pillow and collapse on to it.

She knelt on the floor beside him for a while, murmuring platitudes, stroking his hair. As the sobbing subsided she felt her way round the foot of the bed to the other side, where she lay beside him, reassuring him, kissing his hair. When he turned on his side she was ready for him, clasping herself as closely to him as she could and taking his hand into intimate contact with her body. She sensed the response in him as he shifted into a more comfortable position. She had both arms tightly about him now, crushing him down upon her and searching for his mouth with hers. For one brief instant she found it then he pushed her away and rolled over.

"What the hell are you doing, you whore?"

She lay there as she heard him cross the floor and fumble for the door-handle, still muttering and swearing. She watched as the corridor light came on and he closed the door.

"You fool, you fool," she said to herself. "What have you done?"

Her feelings of remorse were interrupted by banging and hammering on a door which she quickly realised was not hers.

"Whore! Whore! Come on out. I know you're in there." André was shouting, swearing, crying, kicking and hammering at his uncle's door. "Damn you, you bitch, you whore."

Then she heard Albert's stern voice, "But you are drunk, my nephew. You have drunk too much. Go to bed. You are waking everyone up."

"Liar, liar. I'm not drunk. Let me go, let me go. How can you do this to my father and to Auntie Monique. What the hell are you doing? Where's my mother? The whore, the bitch!"

"Don't you dare speak about your mother like that. Calm down. You're drunk. I'm sorry, sir, for this disturbance. The young man is rather the worse for wear, I'm afraid. Ah, young people! It's all right, Anne Sophie, go back to bed. Your cousin is drunk. He'll be all right in the morning."

"I want my mother!" André's voice was high-pitched now, like a lost child's. "Let me in. I want to see her."

"Hush now, André, my son. Why all this noise? Help, Albert, hold him, he's mad."

The shouting moved off along the corridor and down the stairs out of ear-shot. A number of doors closed as disturbed hotel guests returned to their beds.

The English woman lay on her back, eyes wide in the darkness, her body trembling. She was awake when a car started up and roared through the village. She was awake when a second car did the same. If the first car was André's she could only hope he would drive safely. If the second carried Albert or Sylvie or both, she was past caring what happened to them. She herself was already an accident with the wreckage strewn about her.

During that night she relived her time at the College all those years ago, André's first visit and then the last one, trying to make sense of it all. She was an outsider and always had been. She was glad at that now. But she should not have interfered. André might never have known about his mother. Things might always have gone on as they were but once exposed could not be ignored. And then, she hardly dared bring herself to think of it, there had been André's ultimate rejection. What shame! Nothing would be the same again and certainly not here at Saint-André-sur-Audan. In under eighteen hours she would be on her way home, under seventeen hours, under sixteen hours. Eventually she drifted into a sleep where in her dreams Sylvie was calling her a whore and André had taken her train ticket and thrown it into the Audan. In her attempts to reach it she was taken downstream in the swirling waters, unable to save herself. When she awoke she realised the nightmare of meeting the others was still to come.

It was a sultry day, overcast and heavy, with a threat of thunder. She entered the restaurant with trepidation and sat anxiously at her table. André, she knew, would not be there anyway. Nor was there any sign of Sylvie. She glimpsed Albert in the kitchen but only Anne Sophie and Laurence served at table, in a subdued manner.

After breakfast she went into the village. If she was to be an outsider, she may as well act like one. She entered every shop, looking at scarves and paperweights, wooden toys, leather goods, everything. In fact, it was quite interesting and occupied her mind. She chose a couple of silver necklaces each with a dainty pendant for Laurence and Anne Sophie whose eyes lit up at the unexpected gift.

Lunch was served by Sylvie. Her face was more made-up than usual but it was inscrutable.

'I know about her,' thought the English woman. 'But does she know about me?'

In the afternoon she slept until a crash of thunder echoed down the valley and her bed shuddered. She lay there, listening to the violent rumbling and the lashing rain. There would be no work for Philippe at the building site. The storm would give him a rest, unless of course his own personal storm had broken during the night. If André had gone home to his father, if Sylvie had followed. If, if, if...

She finished her packing, writing her home destination on the label with no little relief.

At dinner, served by Anne Sophie, she managed some soup and chicken and rice; she took a piece of fruit for the journey.

At eight o'clock she said her farewells to the girls. Sylvie and Albert came together to kiss her. So they didn't know she knew about them. That was a blessing. She waited alone in the hotel entrance for Philippe to arrive. When she saw him she was taken aback. The day's sorrows had distorted his face, his eyes were sunken and dull, his cheeks lined. He picked up her luggage with grief-stricken hands.

They drove off into the gloom which had descended with the storm, the silence broken only by an occasional flick of the windscreen wipers and a change of gear as they went up through the series of hairpin bends. The woman did not look back. She had abandoned her memory by the river wall and vowed never to return to claim it.

At the station she kissed Philippe on both cheeks with deep affection and thanked him. The last she saw of him was that of a broken figure, by a lamp-post on the platform, shoulders bowed, staring through her as the train moved off, not returning her wave.

Chapter Eleven

Paul drove me along the deserted winter roads, familiar to me now. Soon would be the turning to Mas Saint-André before the zigzag descent to the valley. Already the anxiety within me tensed my whole body.

Long before we reached the turning there were signs announcing Mas Saint-André Holiday Village and Adventure Park, open April to September. As we approached, I could see, right up to the road, wooden chalets totally out of keeping with the stone houses and *lauze* roofs of former times. At the lane end was a board listing the facilities – summer sports on land and in the air, interactive history centre, bier-garten, fast-food, taxi-train to the Audan bridge.

We descended past the tree-line until the village was in view. Paul stopped the car again and we looked down into the silent landscape. There was no movement. No smoke curled up from the chimneys. We continued downwards and pulled up by the post office. It was shuttered. We turned on to the river-front. The local stores had made way for burger-bars, an English pub, a bingo hall and an amusement arcade. The bureau de tabac was still there though, firmly boarded up, with sandbags outside the door. In fact, sandbags slumped lifeless the length of the shop-fronts, as protection against flooding. They reminded me again of Albert's letter, which I had read so often when I received it that I had known it by heart:

> *Dear Helen,*
>
> *I am writing to you because there are things you ought to know. Things are no longer what they were. Firstly, it is with deep regret that I announce to you the death of my dear brother-in-law, Philippe.*
>
> *You were perhaps the last person to see him alive. He was found the next morning at the building site,*

*hanging from one of the structures. I am deeply sorry
to tell you this. It was a terrible shock for us all.*

*We have not seen André since the funeral. He now
lives somewhere in Montpellier, I believe, and studies
at the Faculty. He does not contact us.*

*I must tell you also that Monique no longer lives
here. She is living in Pradoux with all the children. I
am in the process of selling the hotel here and buying
another one near the coast. Sylvie and I will run it
together.*

*Not many hours after Philippe was found, the
Audan rose with all the water from the rain in the
mountains and we had some of the worst floods in the
valley this century. The cellar of our hotel was flooded
and the water was a metre high in some of the shops.
Also, the river destroyed the foundations of the new
hotel complex. The force of it moved great concrete
slabs downstream.*

*I am sorry this is such a sad letter. We are trying to
come to terms with everything.*

Sylvie joins me in affectionate regards,

Albert

The very recollection of the letter filled me with pain. I needed to be
alone, so I sent Paul off to explore on foot the steep alleys of the
village while I crossed the road to the river wall, looking down at the
Audan flowing fast and free beneath me and swirling and tumbling
though the arch of the bridge. Then I held on to the wall and looked in
the other direction, to the Hotel de l'Audan. Only it was not a hotel
any more. According to the sign it was "Butterfly Holiday
Apartments". Huge plastic butterflies were poised on the old stone. A
broken notice advertised in English "Live Musi Nightl Dance till
Daw". By the wall, an orange tarpaulin covered the long taxi-train,
resembling a caterpillar.

I scanned the windows to seek the room where I had last been with
André. The renovations had altered the shape of the building making it
impossible. But the memory was there all the same to ravage my
conscience and to dig its teeth deep into wounds I thought had healed.
The hotel had gone; Albert, Sylvie, Monique all gone, maybe long

since dead; the children, André, all gone. And Philippe, poor Philippe. If only I had broken the silence on the journey to the station. If only he had talked. Had he known my part in his sorrow? What had André said to him?

I slowly passed the Butterfly Holiday Apartments and made my way out of the village. The Audan was wider here than it had been, claiming the very site of the proposed hotel and leisure complex. Well, Philippe would have approved of that, at any rate.

"Hey, Helen!"

I turned and for a split second saw Philippe coming towards me, that same stride, that same tilt of the long head, the same black hair.

"There you are. I wondered where you'd got to."

My godson Paul came to me and I put my hand on his shoulder, knowing he would put an affectionate arm around me, which he did. He so resembled his grandfather and would never know. His mother, Stephanie, and I had made sure of that.

The truth is best left unsaid.

"Fascinating village," said Paul, "with lots of tunnels and passages. There's a big casino at the top. Looks as though it might once have been a school."

We stood gazing out across the valley.

"Look at all those old terraces over there," he went on. "Isn't it a shame they are not used any more?"

I nodded, suddenly overcome with weariness.

"I've seen enough," I said. "Take me away."